CALL ME DANICA

by
Winifred Madison

FOUR WINDS PRESS   NEW YORK

FOR GRETA KOS

By the same author

Maria Luisa
Max's Wonderful Delicatessen
Growing Up in a Hurry
Bird on the Wing
Becky's Horse

LIBRARY OF CONGRESS CATALOGING IN PUBLICATION DATA

Madison, Winifred.
  Call me Danica.

  SUMMARY: A young girl and her family move from a small Croatian village to Vancouver and have many problems adjusting to a new culture.
  [1. Emigration and immigration—Fiction. 2. Canada—Fiction] I. Title.
PZ7.M2652Dan   [Fic]   76-48243
ISBN 0-590-07463-6

Published by Four Winds Press
A Division of Scholastic Magazines, Inc., New York, N.Y.
Copyright © 1977 by Winifred Madison

Library of Congress Catalog Card Number: 76-48243

1 2 3 4 5   81 80 79 78 77

Notes on Pronunciation

The words look strange. Do not be alarmed by the profusion of *j*s, which are pronounced as *y*. The *c* is often pronounced *ch*, as in *child,* or *ts* as in *cats*.

DANICA	is pronounced	Da′-ni-tsa
MIRJANA		Mi′-ri-a-na
MARIJA		Ma-ri′-a
TANJA		Tah′-nya
NADA		Nah′-dya
PAVELIC		Pah′-ve-lich
IVO (John)		Ee′-vo
PJEVAJ (Sing!)		Pi′-a-vy
DOBRO JUTRO		Do-bro Oo′-tro
(Good morning)		(the *j* is silent)
DOBAR DAN		Do-bar Dahn
(Good afternoon)		
SDRAVO		Stra-vo
(Hello or good-bye)		
HLAVA		Hla-vah
(Thank you)		
ZIVALEE		Zhee-vah-lee
(Hooray! This is sometimes spelled *Zivili*)		
TAMBOURA		Tam-bou-rah
(A musical instrument something like a lute. Sometimes spelled *tambura*.)		

MAMO (Mother) is used when speaking directly to a mother; but when one is speaking about her, *Mamo* becomes *Mama*.

CHAPTER 1

Another postcard came from Canada, from Vancouver, the city where Uncle Ivo and Aunt Nevenka lived. My mother shrugged her shoulders as if this card had nothing to do with her and gave it to me casually. Of all the cards and pamphlets they had sent us, this showed the most unbelievable and beautiful of scenes. Vancouver at night appeared to be an island of high towers with squares of golden lights streaming from the windows, and all of this was reflected in bright shimmering water while the ocean in back of the towers danced with the bright lights. To think of living in such a place . . .

"Danica, there's no point in your dreaming. We aren't going there. That's it. We simply aren't going. And don't show off your postcards. It's not nice to boast, even if your aunt and uncle do live there," Mama said.

"I have to show this one to Tanja, Mamo, just this one and then I'll put it away with the others," I promised.

I ran over to Tanja's house. She was sitting in the backyard letting her long black hair dry in the afternoon sun. Dreaming. I've never seen such a dreamer. She watched a bee buzz around some flowers.

"Hey, Tanja, I've got another card. This one's a beauty.

I've even decided where I'm going to live, right here, on top of the highest building. They call it a penthouse. You can come and visit me."

"I will, Danica, I will!" She replied so positively that anyone would think we were moving to Vancouver the very next day to stay there forever. Tanja reached over to pluck a daisy head and pulled the petals off one by one.

"See, it comes out yes! You'll be going and I'll visit you."

I laughed, but she was serious. She took my hand and examined the lines of my palm. "The hand does not lie. See this long travel line? It *proves* you'll be going there. I'll visit you in Vancouver and you can visit me in Zagreb."

Zagreb, the capital city of Croatia, was little more than an hour's travel from Kalovar. It was more likely I'd visit her there than that she'd see me in Vancouver. My father would never leave Croatia. Never.

"I'll see you in Zagreb, of course. My father took me there once to the Opera House. What a place! Lots of stores and restaurants. And we'll be dancing there at the Folk Festival this year."

I was trying to make her feel better about the city she had chosen, but it was still Vancouver for me! I spread my cache of postcards on the grass, views of that amazing city: high blue mountains topped with snow to the north of the city, a bay of blue water dotted with sailboats leaning in the wind, a beach filled with young people, a street of shops, and a bridge with the romantic name, the Lion's Gate Bridge, that seemed to be made of a delicate filigree of wire stretched high above the water. "Tanja, I shall never rest until I see that wonderful city."

In Croatia it was spring. Flowers of all colors literally covered the hillsides. In the distance a flock of sheep

2

grazed on a hilly pasture and across the way a woman sang as she folded the sheets that had been drying on the clothesline.

Lado me milo lade
Lade mi milo lade oj

Vjera sang clearly in a rich, vibrant voice this old song we had heard so often, but I was not impressed. She was always singing.

"C'mon over to my house, Tanja, and let's hear some rock." It was the newest music we craved, the songs from England, Canada and the States. We fell in love with them, writing down the words and singing along as well as we could, though most of the time we didn't know what the songs meant. The English we learned at school didn't prepare us for this new music with its strong use of words. "Ba-by, ba-by," we sang, finally figuring out such a song was not about a baby at all, but a young man's pet name for a girl.

We sang to each other softly, knowing better than to try to impress our parents with the new music. *"Mi smo Hrvati* (We are Croats!), and there is nothing in the world more beautiful than the songs of your own people. Sing those, Danica!" my father said sternly more than once. He was a proud man.

"But she's just a child," Mama said all too often, thinking she was defending me. "She will grow out of it in time."

This remark made me even more furious than my father's lectures. Still Tanja and I twisted the dials of the radio in hopes of hearing snatches of songs from all the new, exciting pop singers.

"I'd go home with you, Danica, only I'm too lazy to go anywhere," Tanja yawned, stretching out on the grass.

Light played around the edges of her firm round cheeks and high forehead. Together we looked up into the clear blue sky through the new green leaves of a pear tree. Bees buzzed around the sweet white flowers of the bush that is called "bridal bouquet" in English. In the fields the red and pink poppies vibrated in the breeze.

"I'm as lazy as you," I admitted as I forced myself to get up. "Only I've GOT to go." Soon it would be dinner at the Inn, and it was my job to wash down the tables, put on the tablecloths, wipe the glasses, a hundred boring things like that.

On the way home I met Jure, a boy at school, twelve years old like me.

"Aren't you off to Canada *yet?*" he teased me.

I stuck out my tongue, though it was my own fault if he made fun of me. It was only recently that I found enough sense not to bring the postcards to school and smile in a superior way when the teacher showed the class a picture of the shore along English Bay with its high, white towers and said reverently, "It's a Northern Riviera, a beautiful place." That was six months ago, but Jure was still making fun of me.

"Come on, Danica, I was only fooling," he said.

Even so, I gave him what my mother calls "the look that burns."

"Anyway, I'd miss you, I guess, if you left," he said shyly and then held out a bag of cherries. "Here, have some. But don't be a pig."

How succulent they looked, dark, red and shining, like sweet little globes. I could have eaten all of them, but I was careful to take only two. "Thanks, Jure, I'd like to talk, but I have to get home."

"Sure, some time come by and see my new little goats."

He was not so bad, I was thinking. I liked goats too, and their new kids.

At home my father was standing on a ladder as he tied up some grapevines that had come loose from the arbor that shaded the terrace. In summer we put tables on the terrace so that the customers could eat under the shade of the grape leaves. Even now we had one table out at the far corner of the terrace where six old men of the village sat and argued politics. In Croatia there is never any end to political discussions. But my father was singing as he worked, an indefinite song full of dum-de-dums and an occasional word, and the voice which strained through his thick black mustache was strong. He was a big man, tall and straight as a pine. Black hair, black eyebrows that jutted over fierce, dark eyes and a straight, strong back under the linen shirt with its decorations of red cross-stitching, he looked like a hero, which was fitting, because he was well known for his bravery in the war.

Now that I saw he was in a good mood, it would not hurt to ask him once more about Canada. Who knows, maybe he had changed his mind since the last time.

"Hey, Papa," I said. "Today we had another postcard from Uncle Ivo."

"And so?" he asked, singing away.

"He says it's a great place there. And he wrote Mama that taxes are bad but not half as bad as here. The restaurant business is very good there, lots of restaurants. He thinks we would get rich there."

The humming stopped. My father put down the twine and shook his forefinger at me, one decisive shake, and I knew what was coming.

"Danica, Danica!"

When he says my name like that, "Danica, Danica," it means a long serious lecture. He came down from the ladder, sat on a wooden chair and pointed to the one where I was to sit and not move until I heard what he had to say. Why do I talk so much, I groaned to myself.

"Daughter, what goes on in that mind of yours? For the last time I shall explain why we stay here in Kalovar, this little village, and then I don't want to hear the word *Canada* or *Vancouver* again. Croatia is an old country; our ancestors came here in the sixteenth century. We had one of the first parliaments in Europe. We are a proud and fiery people with a history that is heartbreaking, yet full of dignity. Time after time we have been overrun by the Venetians, the Hungarians, the Austrians, and remember it was the Croatians who kept the Turks from taking over Europe. Even in my lifetime, it was the Germans, the Italians and then the Russians who came to crush us, and we never gave in. Most of us fought bravely and we still fight. Is it all for nothing, that we should skip off to Canada? Should we leave these lands where your ancestors have lived for so many generations? Danica, I am a son of this soil and you are my daughter. It is here we belong."

"All right, Papa," I said meekly. There was no arguing with him at all. He spoke poetically with deep feeling and picturesque phrases just as though he were giving a speech. As a matter of fact, he loved to become the orator and often preached to the citizens of Kalovar who applauded him or even to the guests of the Inn, who were invariably impressed. Now that I sat submissively, he came down from his imaginary pedestal and talked to me like a father.

"It's like this, Danica. When something is far away, it seems wonderful, but it's only an illusion. When you get there, you find the world is pretty much the same everywhere. People are people. Life is never easy anywhere. If your aunt and uncle and even your cousin, Marija, are happy, well and good, I do not grudge them that. But we belong here. This is our home."

"I guess so," I said. Then he laughed as if once all this nonsense about going to Canada were over, I was not such a bad daughter after all.

"Come, Danica, it's getting late. Better go help Mama set the tables so that we'll be ready when the tour bus comes," he said.

He kissed me and I left.

Late that afternoon I milked the goats as usual. I placed the pail under Snowball, the white goat that was my favorite, and as I milked her with my head next to her warm little body, I dreamed of Vancouver with longing and sadness, as though I had just lost it. I came back to Kalovar in time to catch a mischievous look in Snowball's eye, and snatched the pail away from her just before she would have kicked it over.

"What a devil you are!" I said, and yet I must admit, I loved her.

"Maybe my father is right. Maybe he's not," I mused to Kolo, the little brown goat, named after a dance because she was so lively, "but one thing is sure. He will never leave this place."

Despite my thoughts of Vancouver, I could not help but love Kalovar in the spring. The air was sweet with the odor of honeysuckle, and the bees that hummed around it promised a good yield of honey that year. My father sometimes said that "the air was like a kiss." What more could I want? Yet the doves that flew in the fig tree to each other seemed to coo, "VanCOUver, VanCOUver, VanCOUver!"

The milking finished, I brought the full pail to the house and then climbed to the loft in the room where I slept. I tied the postcards with a length of red yarn and placed them in the carved wooden chest my father once bought for me. This was where I kept mementos and souvenirs: the red and white cap my grandmother had knit for me when I was a very tiny little girl, a book of Croatian poetry I won as a prize at school, the apron and cap I was embroidering to wear at the Folk Festival, an old straw doll. And now this collection of postcards.

I shut the lid and would have locked the chest if I'd had a key.

CHAPTER 2

"Don't forget. There's an extra tour bus today," Tata, my father, reminded us all at breakfast.

It was summer now and school was over. I had hoped to go over to Tanja's, but now I knew I'd have to help Mama in the kitchen all morning. I knew enough to keep my mouth shut and not complain or I'd receive scoldings from both my mother and father. Though the people of Kalovar use the Inn for parties and the men like to sit around and argue for hours, it is the tour buses stopping on their way to Zagreb all through the summer that bring us our income.

"We are so lucky," Mama would say as though this were a Divine and Happy Accident, "that Kalovar is on the way to Zagreb."

If the tourists remember Kalovar at all, it is probably "that sleepy little town where we stopped at that charming inn for lunch!" And if my sister, Mirjana, and I remember the tourists at all, it is for the same questions that they asked over and over in Croatian impossible to understand, or French, or German or English. Eventually we learned to understand what they were trying to say, no matter the language.

"What's this?" they ask pointing to the menu and choking over the names of the various dishes. *Gulas, čevapčiči, kackavalj* . . . they strain their tongues trying to pronounce our terms for goulash or stew, little meat balls, sheep's cheese. Then they eye one another questioningly until at last the food appears; in the end they are always won over by Mama's superb cooking.

The second question always is, "What is there to see in Kalovar?" The first time I heard this I looked to Mirjana for the answer. She shrugged her shoulders. What is there to see? One could enjoy looking at the green fields, or the golden strips of wheat, or the vineyards. The river that runs through the village is so small it is not named, yet it rushes vigorously and fish can be caught there. In the distance sheep can be seen grazing in pastures, leafy green trees in summer and always the evergreens which point sharply into the blue sky. Is that not enough? No, the tourists appear disappointed. They were hoping to find an ancient church or a bit of choice folk art they could take home.

The third question always is this: "What do you do with yourself in such a quiet place?" We live, that is what we do, I want to answer. We go to school in winter, do our chores in summer, go to church on Sundays and dance when we can. What kind of foolish question is that?

But we were always polite and acted honored no matter what kind of nonsense we had to listen to. This was our Inn and we had pride in it. It was also our living and we were not allowed to complain, lest "the angels overhear and punish us by taking it away."

That day was like any other. At noon Mirjana and I changed from our ordinary clothes to old peasant blouses with full sleeves and low, square necks, full blue skirts and aprons covered with embroidery. Mirjana found old embroidered headdresses which she thought we should use even though women had not worn such things for ages. We did not wear our best dresses, which we reserved for special occasions such as weddings and holidays and festivals.

"How lovely you girls look!"

"*Très joli!*"

"Please, could we have your photograph?"

It had happened before. Even before we could seat the visitors from the tour bus, we posed for them, smiling prettily, and then we showed them to their tables, outside in the shade of the grapevines or inside where the thick walls kept the room cool. My father welcomed everyone as though it were his personal dining room, and we felt a familiar buzz of appreciation.

As we took the orders, again explaining *čevapčiči* and *sogan dolma,* I noticed that one of the women wore a pin in the shape of a maple leaf on the collar of her pantsuit.

"You are Canadian?" I asked slowly in my best English.

At first she did not understand me, but when I repeated the question she nodded.

"I would like very much to go to Canada," I said.

"Really," she said dismissing my dream as she turned to talk with her companion. How disappointing that they seemed so dull and indifferent! I expected more of Canadians. But then they looked up at me beaming; it took me a few minutes to understand they were complimenting us on having indoor plumbing and that it was clean!

"You should not have conversations with guests," Mirjana scolded me as I stood in the kitchen beside her, cutting Mama's wonderful plum cake into serving pieces. I could not help but feel disappointed, that two women should come halfway around the world and talk about nothing more than how wonderful it is that the toilet is clean. I was about to tell Mirjana when we heard tinkling bells in the road, and Mirjana flashed a look at me from her long, black lashes.

"That monkey is at it again. Papa shouldn't let him go on like that. Marko is so spoiled."

"Don't be silly. Papa adores him. He thinks that's cute."

I didn't have to look out of the window to know what was happening. Marko, my eight-year-old brother, was leading half a dozen goats, each with a bell around its neck, down the road. Nobody looked more the picturesque shepherd than Marko in the red knitted cap and a vest he borrowed from Vlado, who is a real shepherd. Immediately all the guests grabbed their cameras and rushed outside to "catch this remarkable find."

Marko, that imp, regarded them blankly, as though he couldn't imagine what they wanted, nor had ever seen a camera before. He appeared to be on the verge of driving the goats (which did not even belong to him but to Vlado) down the road, when a man rushed up to him, put a few coins in his hand and explained with exaggerated gestures that they wanted him to stand still for a moment. A master at posing, Marko stood soberly as the goats gathered around him. Then a lady stepped forward and tried to communicate that she wanted him to smile, and after she pressed a few more coins in his hand, he brightened, suddenly understanding her. He grinned, almost swaggeringly, as he posed proudly with one hand on his hip, and as more coins were given to "that dear shepherd boy," Mirjana and I wiped the sweat from our foreheads as we rushed to get the desserts ready to serve.

"Mamo, that's disgraceful," Mirjana cried, "and it's not

fair. They never pay us for posing, and Marko doesn't even work."

"I know," Mama agreed, "but that's how it is when you're a woman. You get the worst of it."

Mirjana and I exchanged bitter looks, but we smiled as we entered the dining room to serve coffee and cake. The tourists beamed happily now because of the pictures they took of this "dear sleepy little town." We thanked our guests as they boarded the bus while they praised us and promised to come back sometime, but our smiles faded after the bus bounced away and we were left with twelve tables full of dishes that had to be washed and a floor that had to be swept.

My father collected all the tips and then gave Mirjana and me our "wage," which wasn't much. But then it was always like that in Kalovar. We didn't know enough to be greedier than we were.

He went to work in his garden, my mother returned to the house to make the bread for the next day, and Mirjana and I were left to clean up.

"What's the matter with you?" Mirjana asked. "Did someone hurt your feelings?"

"It's the tourists," I said. "They are nice enough, but do you suppose all Canadians are like that lady? Those two reminded me of cows that have to be herded around. Do you suppose they're all like that in Canada?"

"They *are* very nice," Mirjana said, "but they're tourists, that's all. Some of them are dull, but anyway, we don't have to worry what people are like in Canada or anywhere else because we aren't going anywhere."

"They seem so surprised because everything is clean and Mama cooks well and we are all dressed up to be so quaint. Blah! I'm going swimming, soon as I get the floor done."

Hot and discouraged I put the last of the clean dishes away, washed the floor and was ready to leave when the cowbell over the door tinkled its pleasant sound. A voice of a young person called out:

"Hello, hello, is anybody here?"

Another young voice repeated this in what I guess was meant to be Croatian. *"Dobar dan!"* Good afternoon!

Mirjana and I sighed because the thought of dipping into that cool river had been such a delicious one and now we had guests to take care of, but when we saw that they were three young people, two boys and a girl with long straight hair the color of wheat, we found ourselves inviting them in. They were tired and dusty, yet they grinned at us as they collapsed on chairs around a table.

"Please come in," I said in my best English, although it was a little foolish because they had already made themselves at home.

The boy with the short dark hair spoke for the group, a mixture of English and Croatian with a few Greek words thrown in. It did not matter; we understood one another. All three young people wore backpacks and were dressed alike in jeans, dusty boots and sweat-stained shirts. The second boy carried a guitar.

"Can we get something to eat?" the spokesman asked, and Mirjana gave them menus. The girl sighed, exhausted. The three of them slouched in their chairs, legs spread out in front of them, and we guessed they had been walking for a long time. And yet they were wonderful, I could not say why. Perhaps it's the way they smiled, the way they looked at us directly, not as if we were some quaint peasants to be photographed but real people; or perhaps it's because they seemed to be doing something I would have loved doing.

We served them some of Mama's good soup, and the girl invited us to sit down with them. Mirjana and I hesitated; one does not sit down with guests; but suddenly that rule seemed ridiculous. These were three people who appeared to be interested in us, and Mirjana, as much as I, wanted to know all about them, who they were and where they came from.

"English? American?"

Eventually, with each of them explaining in several languages and with any number of gestures, we learned that the blond boy was Canadian . . . from Quebec and the other couple was from California. They explained they were traveling through Yugoslavia and Greece, sometimes hiking, or hitchhiking, or bicycling and, now and then, taking a bus.

"And your parents let you do this?" Mirjana asked, shocked, knowing that ours would never permit it, even though Mirjana was seventeen and our visitors were not much older. Watching them, I vowed someday I would be footloose and free, no matter what Mama and Tata had to say about it.

"Let's make a special plate for them," Mirjana said when we were in the kitchen, so we made up "sampling dishes" with a little of this and a little of that. It pleased them, and the boy from Canada may have been flirting with Mirjana, though she sat in her chair reserved and even standoffish.

"Would you sing for us?" I asked when they were through eating.

"Sure, what do you want to hear?"

"Anything. Everything. Country music I like very much. And all the latest singers."

I mentioned them, but could not have pronounced them well for it took three repetitions for them to understand. Still, I felt sophisticated to know about these singers.

The boy named Larry took out his guitar and they all

sang along with him; at one point he played a Beatles tune and I surprised them by singing along with them.

"Hey, do you know this one? It's really old," Larry said, and he played a folk song I'd never heard before, "On Top of Old Smoky." Mirjana, reserved as she was, fell in love with that song and begged for more.

"I've had it. I'm bushed," Larry said after three more songs. "It's time you sang for us. Would you? Some Croatian songs?"

Mirjana understood what he asked and did not hesitate to sing, not because she was immodest but it seemed only polite to answer a song with a song. Now Mirjana is not a very big person and at first glance she appears quiet and mild, not in the least dramatic. And so they were surprised when she sang, for her voice is powerful, high and clear, like that of a woman working in one field and singing to her lover who is a mile away. She sang a love song:

> *Marice moja, Marice moja,**
> *Marice moja, sweetheart mine,*
> *Do you still, O still, remember*
> *How with your white arms above*
> *Lifted up as though to clasp me*

And so it goes, on and on for five verses.

To tell the truth, I thought it silly of her to choose such a song, but she signaled to me to join her and so I did. My voice is like hers because we often sing together when we are working in the Inn and can't think of anything to talk about. When we finished the song, they applauded.

"What voices, what a beautiful song!"

"Will you teach us?"

"Sing some more."

(* It is pronounced Ma-rit-za mo-ya)

The afternoon passed like a dream that was intensely sweet. We could not talk much, limited by our knowledge of each other's language, yet it did not matter. Soon they were singing some of our songs and Mirjana and I learned a Western song, "Git Along Little Dogies," and a mountain song, "Down in the Valley." We forgot that it was hot, that we meant to go swimming but now it was too late, that we felt sorry for ourselves because Marko made a nice pile of coins with his little trick while we worked most of the day for very much less and that many of the people we served saw us as only a convenience on their trip or something picturesque, good for a snapshot, but not as people. All that was changed now. When the afternoon was over, Mirjana agreed that for us it was almost like traveling to America.

The girl looked at her watch and asked when the bus left, for they were due in Zagreb that night. They paid for dinner; Mirjana insisted they take some buns with them and some of the fine plums that grow in our orchard, and we walked with them to the place where the bus stops when it is flagged down.

"Good-bye, thank you, thank you," they cried to us as they left. They waved to us and we waved to them until they were out of sight.

"Someday," I told Mirjana, "we will take a bus and leave this place, for America."

She shook her head as though I would never learn, but this time she did not scold me. We sang "On Top of Old Smoky" all the way back to the Inn.

CHAPTER 3

Jure came by one afternoon with one of his baby goats. Nothing in the world is as dear as a young goat, but this one was sad, for his leg had met with an accident and it stuck away from his thigh at an abnormal angle.

"I don't know how it got broken," Jure said, "poor little kid. Maybe a horse stepped on it, I really don't know. But you can fix it. You've fixed so many poor animals."

The kid baaed pitifully even though I hardly touched his broken leg.

"It will have to be reset," I said, sounding solemn and wise although anyone at all knew that.

"Dr. Pavelic, you have the job!" he said.

I snorted, yet I liked the sound of it. Dr. Pavelic!

"Really, Danica, you have many admirers. Ivo told me how you cured his sick lamb even when the vet gave up on it. And all the kids know that you can fix birds with broken wings, broken legs; you cured Pedja's cat, Tanja's cat; you stopped the bleeding on Stanko's dog that time when he was caught on a wire fence . . ."

"Stop, Jure. I don't know anything. And I've had a few failures too. But you could do as well, even better, if you wanted. I know, you're busy with that big herd of yours."

Usually Jure and I exchanged insults; today we progressed to compliments and it was just as much a contest to see who could "pile it on" the most. "I know you'll be able to fix her," he said and took off.

"What am I going to do with you?" I asked the pitiful creature who kept baaing in pain. It was a curious break, one I had not encountered before. I could understand a simple break and had had luck in resetting the broken limbs of several crippled animals and seeing them get well again. But this was not a simple case as the others had been.

"I tell you what, sweet little goat. We'll go see Vesna."

I carried the bleating animal down the hill, through the street that ran through the village, past the school, past the church, past the priest who greeted us; then I turned left and walked up a grassy path that wound over a hill and came to rest in a grove of birch trees. It seemed to stop there, but I knew the secret of a hidden path that led to an opening where a small hut stood. Drying herbs and strings of red peppers decorated the outside, and smoke rose through the small twisted chimney that corkscrewed from the thatched roof. A parrot in a large cage built of rushes shrieked *Dobro jutro* over and over.

"Silly bird," I said. "It's way past morning."

A sweet grassy odor I could not identify penetrated the air, and I wondered what brew Vesna was making this time. Some of the village people whispered that she was a witch and no wonder, with her bent back, the strands of gray hair stuck out from her straggly bun of hair, and the long nose and chin which promised to meet someday. But her eyes were remarkably blue, clear and compassionate, so that I never could see her as anything but a good spirit. I did not mind that she smelled of garlic, which she vowed kept her from catching cold, and that she could have posed for an illustration in a book of fairy tales in her old-fashioned long skirt and shawl as she stood before her hovel. I knew of no better doctor.

"Vesna!" I shouted, for she was a trifle deaf.

She turned from the black pot-bellied stove where she concentrated on stirring something in a thick earthenware pot.

"Danica, my little one, come in, come in."

The kid bleated as though to announce his misery.

"And you, I didn't see you at first. My poor suffering little sweet. Little one, let me look at you."

"It's Jure's goat. I can't seem to figure out how to mend his foot. It's awfully out of shape."

"A big creature must have stepped on him. There, it's broken here and, let me see, yes, down here again. So many complications for such a tiny creature. See Danica, first we must set this. . . ."

Taking a piece of charcoal, she drew the joints on a piece of board so that I could see what had happened and what must be done. A witch indeed! No hocus-pocus here, no magic spells.

Vesna cleared the table, gathered some sticks, quickly shaved them smooth and laid out bindings of linen that were clean but old.

"Are you ready now, Danica? There, you can hold the little fellow, if you will."

I put the terrified animal on the table and held him securely while Vesna expertly manipulated his leg. She knew exactly what to do; it took less than a minute, and before the goat let out its agonized bleat, she was already wrapping the splint and bandage around the damaged limb.

"Vesna, what a genius you are! I would give anything to know as much as you."

"Come and I shall teach you. Now you know how to set a leg even when it's badly fractured like this."

I did not think I would come across many such twisted limbs. When I thought of all the things Vesna could do, my head reeled. She had brought ever so many babies into the world, even the most difficult births; she had cured children of fevers, given herbs to help all sorts of ailments; hardly a person in the village was not grateful to her for one kind of cure or another. And yet the doctor from the next village was always called first, for it was rumored that Vesna was part gypsy and that nobody really knew where she came from. She had no family.

The kid was quiet now and Vesna put him in the grass where he lay contentedly, nibbling bits of green here and there.

"And now, have some soup with me, Danica. It is a summer soup made with the most remarkable herbs. They will make you even prettier than you are now."

Together we sat on the stoop of her hut as we lunched on soup. The air was filled with remarkable odors, the drying herbs, the grass, the sweet smell of summer sunlight, and along with it a whiff of Vesna's ever-present garlic.

"So you want to be a healer, do you?" she asked.

"Yes, a doctor. But I'd also like to sing in a café, in a city. I like to dance." I had often imagined myself wearing a slinky black dress and singing into a microphone in a sophisticated bar.

"Let me see your hand," Vesna said. My hand was going to get worn out with people reading it, but I let her have it. "Just as I thought, no black dress for you, no cafés. You will be good doctor."

"I don't have to make up my mind yet, do I?" I asked, visualizing myself in a white coat walking down a hospital corridor. I rather liked that picture too.

"Do you want to study with me, yes or no?" Vesna asked, very serious now. "Because if you do, I will teach you much, those things that you will not learn at a medical college. It is wrong to laugh at the old folk remedies, because there is wisdom in them. That is the truth. I know it. I can teach you what I know, if you want to learn."

"There is so much to learn," I said, glancing at the rows of bottles and bags of herbs and baskets of strange objects in her hut.

"When you are ready, come," Vesna said. "And thank you for coming today. You are not silly like most young girls."

"I'm not?" I asked innocently, knowing I could roll on the floor for hours in a fit of laughter.

"Here, I'm busy now, but you take this, Danica," she said, giving me some black, sweet, leaf-shaped, gummy objects. "That is a licorice I made from herbs, good for your blood. And it tastes good too."

"Thanks, Vesna, for this, and mostly for helping the goat. You are good to teach me."

"Come again. You know better than to be afraid of old Vesna, eh?"

I hugged her. The old woman's eyes sparkled for a minute, then turned grave again. "Don't forget. You have the gift. You must not waste it."

"All right," I promised easily. Then picking up the goat carefully so as not to jar his tender leg, I carried him through the main street of Kalovar back home.

CHAPTER 4

Every time I began to dream of Vancouver, Mama sensed it. "Why torture yourself?" she asked. I think she would gladly have hidden the postcards that still came now and then, one showing a large modern theater and another displaying twelve totem poles, impressive and curious sculptures.

"You never see anything like those in Kalovar," I said.

"Right. It's a wonder that Kalovar has managed to exist for so many centuries without a single totem pole. But what we *do* have is the *Smotra Folklora,* the Folk Dance Festival in Zagreb. And it's an honor that our girls will both be in it this year!"

"H'm!" I acted unconcerned, as though it meant nothing to me, but the truth is when one of the young women in the village dance group moved away and I was asked to take her place, it was heady news. Before that I was just a child. Now I felt grown-up to take part in the Festival.

"It's not that you're such a great dancer," Marko said, determined to prick my pride. "They chose you only because you're tall."

"Brat!" I said, sticking out my tongue. But he was probably right. Tanja danced much better than I, but whereas she was still short, I had shot up tall during the past year. To keep her from feeling hurt over an unfair situation, I had to pretend that I didn't really care at all.

"I'd rather be doing modern dancing, or whatever it is they do in cafés or in the cities. This is such old stuff."

"But it's so beautiful!" she said. "When you turn around, your dresses twirl and everything seems to move. And the music is so exciting. I can't sit still once I hear it."

"Then maybe someday you can take my place," I offered generously, though I wasn't ready to offer it to her this season.

Mama was finishing my dress, staying up nights to work on the hundreds of tiny pleats around the waist, each one of which had to be ironed separately so that when I moved in a circle, the dress would swing out. The skirt was a pure linen, bordered with red stitches in a pattern which belonged to our village alone. The apron over the dress was embroidered with red and golden flowers; the blouse that I wore had full sleeves with insets of lace, set off by a tight red bodice; and on my head a kerchief embroidered with red flowers. Mama made me try on the dress one night. Immediately I began to move, as though I were dancing the *kolo*, which is a lively circle dance.

"How can I fit you when you move around so much?" she complained.

I stood still while she fussed with the seams, and as soon as she finished I twirled around fast to make the dress stand out. It felt glorious.

"See how lucky we are," Mirjana said. "We almost lost these songs and dances. When people here wanted a modern society with factories and cars, they wanted to throw out the old things, like the dances, for everything new.

But it turned out that people from other countries were beginning to appreciate our dances and our songs. Now they come from all over to see us perform."

Soon Mirjana would be making speeches just like Papa. She leaned forward to see herself in the mirror, carefully primping her hair and touching her face with rouge. She admired herself first this way and then that, not realizing that the rest of us were watching her.

"That means Mirko will be there at the rehearsal tonight, all that dolling up and smiling at yourself," Mama teased.

Mirjana tossed her head and changed the subject abruptly. "You'd better get into your other clothes, Danica, and hurry about it or you'll be late."

She swept out of the door, twenty minutes early, but Mama and I knew that that was because Mirko would be there. He was a farmer, a very good farmer—one of the best around, Mama said—and he seemed to be fond of Mirjana. As for Mirjana, that sensible little bird could become quite giddy when she danced with Mirko, who led the program.

The moon was on the horizon as I hurried to the rehearsal, and the musicians were tuning their instruments. We had what was called a *tambourica* band, the *tambourica* being a kind of lute related to the guitar; we also had two violins, a *zurla* which was like an oboe that made a piercing sound, and a two-headed drum called a *tupan*. Even as they tuned their instruments, my feet were impatient to begin. I had worked long in the Inn that day and for a while became tired but now I felt fresh and renewed.

We began with the simpler dances; some of them were very stately and dignified. Then we progressed through the more complicated ones, and if anyone made a mistake,

Mirko made us do it again and again. The villagers were watching us, some of them clapping with the music and urging us on, but one finicky old gentleman, Vlado, saw every mistake, every false move and wagged his fingers at us. He insisted that we had to be perfect if we were to represent *his* village.

The dances grew wilder and wilder. My feet were flying, my hair flung out, and my skirt whirled in rhythm. I did not have to think of putting this foot here or that one there; my feet took care of themselves, and I could feel the blood coursing through my veins. Even though I was out of breath, I could have danced forever, but the music came to a stop and we threw out our arms in triumph.

Now the moon was high in the sky, a hard silvery ball, and suddenly it was late. "We can't dance all night," Mirko announced, "because tomorrow morning will be here soon and the cows will want to be milked. I just can't make them understand how good it is to dance."

Then Mirko said we had to meet again very soon and iron out a few difficulties.

"He's a perfectionist," my father said. He had come down to watch the rehearsal and now we walked home together. "Are you worn out, Danica?"

"No, I've never felt so alive. There's nothing so exciting as this."

"I used to feel that way too. Only when we danced, we used to show off with tricks. . . ." He described these feats, which, I must confess, seemed a little too colorful and exaggerated, but he must have been a marvelous dancer. Even now and then, he cut a caper when he led many of the dances at weddings.

"Do you know why the Croatians dance so well?" he asked.

I groaned. I was in for another lecture, but his eyes were gleaming, so I played my part, asking with wide-eyed innocence, "No, why, Papa?"

"Because for us life is full and zesty. Croatians live fiercely. They are brave, free and strong, and their dancing reflects it. Nowhere else in the world is it as good as it is here."

"Nowhere else? Are you sure of that?" I asked, but his shaggy head was thrown back and I suspect he was dreaming of the dancing he did when he was young, for he hardly seemed to hear me.

CHAPTER
5

Tanja's daisy-petal fortunes and assurance that the lines in my palm *proved* I would get to Vancouver were pleasing, but nothing seemed more unlikely than that they would come true. Yet the course of events which would eventually show she was right began one unhappy day, a week before we were going to perform at the Folk Festival in Zagreb. It was also two days before my thirteenth birthday.

Every second of that day is as clear as though it happened yesterday. At first it seemed an ordinary hot summer day. As usual the roosters crowed, silly birds thinking they made the sun come up. The doves cooed in the grape vines. The branch of a plum tree filled the view from my casement window with rich green leaves and rich purple fruit, all against the background of a burning blue sky.

Mama prepared breakfast as usual. Peaches that had been picked that very morning and still with the tiniest pearls of water on their pink fuzzy skin; a bowl of white yogurt; fresh bread my mother had just baked; a small jar of honey; a pot of tea. As I lingered over my dish of sliced peaches and yogurt, I could see my little brother, Marko, out in the garden helping my father tie carrots in bunches. They had already prepared two boxes of green and yellow squash and filled a large basket with intensely purple eggplant.

"He'd better not take so much," Mama said, looking out of the window. "If he sells everything at market, we won't have enough for the tour bus."

"There's enough, Mamo. Papa knows what he's doing," Mirjana said as she rolled out dough for what would become buttery buns filled with sugar, raisins and nuts. Mirjana looked very much like my mother, not very tall and distinctly feminine with the same patient softness of curves and the same warm golden brown eyes. It was Marko and I who took after Papa, being taller and more slender, quicker in the way we spoke and moved, certainly less sweet and less patient than Mama and Mirjana. Marko's eyes gleamed like Papa's and Mama said mine were just the same, and also that my hair was "rebellious and stubborn," so that she cut a fringe or bangs over my forehead and let the rest of my thick black locks fall to my shoulder. Mirjana's hair was a soft dark brown, obedient hair that let itself be worn in a fat soft knot at the crown of her head, now that she was seventeen. Mirjana was not actually fat, yet sometimes she reminded me of the plump brown hen pheasants that lived in the hedges by the grain fields.

My father came in for breakfast, moving more slowly than he usually did and saying very little. When Mama saw he was not eating much, she asked, "What's the matter, Milo? Don't you like the yogurt? Or don't you feel well?"

"I'm all right," he answered gruffly.

"You look a little white," Mama said.

It seemed to me that he did not look well and that he

29

was pale underneath his ruddy tan, but I said nothing, of course. He broke his roll into pieces but only nibbled at it. Mama made an extra sandwich for his lunch in case he gained his appetite later on. Then it was time for him to leave. We walked outside with him, as we always did. He kissed us all good-bye, though I thought he held me more closely than he ever had before.

"Help Mama now and don't run off to Canada before I get home," he joked with me and then added tenderly, *"Lijepa curica!"* which is Croatian for "pretty girl."

"Can I go with you, *please,* Papa?" Marko was pulling at him, begging as he did every week to let him go to market. Once in a while Papa let him go; more often he barked a decisive NO at poor Marko, but on that day, Marko was lucky.

"It's not a bad idea," Papa said. "It's about time you began to learn something about buying and selling. Isn't that so, Nadja?"

My mother said she supposed so, but she was still worrying because my father looked pale. "Come back soon, Milo," she said, a hint of pleading in her voice which I had never heard before.

Later, as Mirjana and I stood in the kitchen cutting up peaches for preserves and stopping to complain uselessly that it was still another scorching day, I thought about Papa and Marko. "This is how it is, Mir: You're the smart one; I'm the pretty one; but it's always Marko who gets to go to market with Papa, just because he's a boy."

"What's the matter, don't you think I'm pretty too?" she asked unexpectedly, but then she went on as though what I said was right, "Someday Marko will be a man and he has a lot to learn."

"And someday we'll be women. Won't we have a lot to learn too? You'd think that Mama would go with him once in a while, for the fun of it if nothing else."

She did not bother to argue. She liked everything the way it was.

Tanja came over later that morning and we sat in the big room and twisted the radio dials until we could hear very faintly something that could have been popular music. I tried to catch the tune and sing along with it while Tanja frowned a little over the new red pattern she was embroidering on a piece of handspun linen, stitches so tiny she actually counted the number of linen threads allotted to each.

It's going to take you forever to finish that," I told her.

She looked up calmly. "That's all right. There's always enough time."

For reasons I could not understand, that particular phrase shook me, though Tanja was bent over her work again, as calm as ever. I found more music on the radio but listened to it without singing; somehow I didn't feel like singing that morning.

Mirjana called to us to come and have lunch, a cold soup made of spinach leaves, with a dollop of yogurt and a sprinkling of chives, a typical summer lunch. Afterward we all felt like stretching out under the shade of the hickory tree, but Tanja had to go home, and Mirjana and I had to rush to the kitchen to take care of the pot that was full of boiling peach preserves. No sooner did we finish ladling it into jars, when we heard a small commotion outside and Marko came running into the house. "Mama, where's Mama? Quick!"

My mother rushed in from the Inn, where she had been working. "Marko, what is it?" Her face was blanched white even before he told her.

"It's Papa. He's sick."

We rushed outside to find him slumped in the seat of the truck, his face so contorted with pain that it looked like a green mask. We helped him down and let him lean on us as we carried him, as well as we could, into the house. He collapsed on the bed in agony.

"My side, here! Right here!" he grasped, clutching the place that hurt.

Mirjana ran to the telephone in the Inn to call the doctor in the next village, for there was no doctor in Kalovar. Apparently he could not be found, for I heard her calling other places. She came back to the kitchen and whispered to me there, so that my father couldn't hear what she said.

"I could murder that doctor," she said, referring to the one in the next village. "He's gone fishing and left no word so that he can be reached. And in Pauvac the doctor has moved away."

"Vesna, let's get Vesna then," my mother said. "Danica, would you? Tell her to come fast."

I ran down the hot dusty road as fast as I could and prayed that Vesna would know what to do. I was frightened, scared in a way I'd never known before, and helpless. Vesna was our last hope.

I caught her just as she was about to go walking in the forest. Hearing the panic in my voice as I called, she turned and rushed over to me. Breathlessly I explained what happened as she packed a basket with herbs, bottles of mysterious liquids and a small round box. In no time at all I was running up the dusty road to the house with Vesna waddling as fast as she could.

"She'll know what to do," I kept repeating hopefully to myself, but when she saw my father, she shook her head from side to side. He saw the gesture and groaned.

"It's appendix. For this you need a doctor," she said. "But we can make you more comfortable.

"Now Danica, Mirjana, find some clean towels, wring them out in very cold water and place them on his inflamed side. Keep replacing them, as cold as possible. Keep phoning for the doctor." Then just before she left she turned to all of us. "Pray, all of you. Do not stop praying for a minute."

My father nodded thanks for the relief of the cold compresses, though he was still in pain. He moaned and then fell asleep, a short fitful rest. "That's a good sign," Mama said, never leaving his side. But he always woke in greater agony than before.

"Where can that doctor be! Mirjana, keep trying. Please," Mama whispered in a tense, worried voice not at all her usual, calm tone. She would not take her eyes from my father as she sat by him. From time to time she bent over to kiss his forehead, fingering her rosary beads and her lips moving in prayer.

The long stifling afternoon seemed stuck, like a stopped clock. A strange quietness fell over the house, interrupted by the bleat of a goat in a distant pasture, the shrill call of a bird or the distant stridulation of a cricket. Mirjana and I stayed close to one another, and Marko stood near us, waiting and saying nothing. We watched my father who did not sleep so much as he seemed to fall into a daze, only to wake with a sudden jolt of pain. The lids on his eyes were so heavy he could barely lift them. At last my mother turned to me with a sadness in her bearing and she said, "Danica, go get the priest."

He lived at the other end of the village and I was surprised he had not already come, for the news of my father's sudden illness spread, and all along the way, small groups of men and clusters of women stood outside their houses in a hushed, tense waiting. Yet even as I ran past them, I could hear the sheep baaing in the pasture; far away a woman sang as she worked in her garden. A chicken ran in front of me as a rooster chased it across the street. A dog barked. How could the world go on like this as though nothing had happened? How could the sun keep shining? How could Kalovar go on in its sleepy, summery, ordinary way when my father lay in mortal pain?

The priest was on his hands and knees as he weeded his garden, and when I explained why we needed him, he gasped, putting his hands to his lips. "Your father, Danica? But he's strong as an ox, that father of yours. I shall come immediately." He rushed, slipping into his robe as he left the house, and carrying his vial of holy oil; then we ran as fast as we could through the hot and blinding streets of Kalovar. Now a real crowd milled in front of the house, and as we came near and I heard the sound of wailing, I knew I would never see my father alive again.

The priest said some final prayers while the rest of us stood back, too shocked to believe this was happening. And then a white Zastava drove up and the doctor we had been trying to reach all afternoon came in. The crowd stepped back to let him pass. To me he looked like someone who had enjoyed an afternoon's fishing, not a doctor who is supposed to save people's lives. When he saw that he was too late, he said he was sorry.

"Sorry! Sorry! Sorry!"

I wanted to pound him with my fists, kick him all over and scratch out his eyes. As if this were not bad enough, that he actually had been fishing, he had the gracelessness to remark to my father's brother, who stood there weeping, "It's really a tragedy," as if we did not already know this. "It's only a burst appendix. Had he only come to me sooner, I could have saved him. Really, it's such a simple operation, nothing to it."

Then I knew I was going to rush at him to kick him, punch him and tear at his eyes, but Mirjana understood and held me back. "It won't do any good. I know how you feel. But it's over now. Over."

Now the house was filled with our friends and people from the village, many of them weeping and shaking their heads in disbelief. My mother did not cry but sat stunned beside my father, as if she could not understand what had happened. Neither Mirjana, Marko nor I wept, but stood immobile as if caught in a bad dream. Only my father seemed to be at peace. His body lay relaxed as though he were sleeping. From time to time my mother touched his cheek and then looked around.

"He's cold," she announced.

"He will have a hero's funeral," I heard a woman say, and some men grunted in agreement. I heard phrases, "a great man," "a true Croat," "there was never a better man."

This house full of wailing people was a nightmare. How could I not believe that my father would come striding through the door as he usually did on market days at just this time of day when the sun was beginning to drop behind the hills? I could almost hear his bass voice booming, "Well, well, what's going on here? You'd think someone had died."

Then a new kind of wailing arose in the distance, a long drawn-out chorus of baaing as the goats complained that nobody had come to milk them. What a relief it was to leave the house, grateful that even my father's death would not keep the sweet milk from filling the udders of the animals. As I leaned my head against the soft white fur of Snowball's ribs, I could hear her heart beating, and as the milk filled the pail with its usual swishing sound, it comforted me to know that life went on anyway, even though my father had died. As I finished milking Snowball and went on to the next goat, she pranced cff gracefully to nibble at a blade of succulent grass, then looked back at me wonderingly as if to ask what had happened. She knew something was different, yet she did not understand.

"I don't understand it either," I told her. One woman had kept repeating "It's God's will, God's will," and that I understood least of all.

When the milk was put away, I could not bear to stay in the grief-laden house and so ran to a grove of pine trees where I could be alone. Now I stretched out on the piney ground and beat it with my fists while deep dry sobs shook me apart.

"I'll never see him alive again. I'll never see him again!" Saying the words did not make it any easier to believe them.

A hero's funeral! But such an indignity, to die of a burst appendix! My father, who truly was a hero—ask any citizen of Kalovar or of all the province for that matter—had hidden in the hills during the wars to fight all invaders, to defeat the traitors, and drive out our enemies. He had been shot, had once been stabbed, had nearly drowned on another occasion, and yet he survived. It was my father who insisted on rebuilding Kalovar, which had been ravaged during the war. No man was more admired or loved. He should have lived to be a hundred years old. Instead, something that could have been simply handled by the twist of a surgeon's knife, that unnecessary part of him, the appendix . . . had ended his life.

Why had I not known what to do? I should have recognized that something was wrong that morning and not let it go as though I weren't aware of it. I stopped sobbing and began to think. I no longer blamed the doctor but myself for not sensing the seriousness of his pallor that morning; I could always tell when the animals were ill, but I could not imagine that anything would ever happen to my strong invincible father. How many times had I fixed the broken limbs of a sheep or goat, or cured a sick cat or even nursed back to life young birds that had fallen from their nests. Vesna had faith in me. Even my father once said I had the gift of healing when he had given up on a sick calf but I took care of it and brought it back to health. Yet I had failed my father when he needed me.

I stopped pounding the earth and sat up straight. For the first time in my life, I made a vow. I would become a doctor. My father was beyond saving, but I would make up for his death by saving others. No sooner did I realize this, than it was clear I had already known this was what I would do. My father used to say, "Danica, Danica, what will you do with your life? What will become of you?"

"How would I know?" I answered, puzzled.

"Well, you are still a child," he would answer, "go and play." It was always a relief to skip away.

Now that he was no longer there, I knew the answer to his question. If only I could have told him. I could practically see him considering my decision, nodding his head gravely and approving it.

"Yes, Danica," he would say, "that is something worthwhile, something very good indeed."

In the time that I sat alone under the pine trees, I became calm, knowing that the direction of my life had changed and would never again be as it was before. Then I went back to the house to see if I could comfort Mama.

On the day that my father was given a hero's funeral, with the drums beating slowly and all the villagers dressed in black following in a solemn procession, I became thirteen years old.

CHAPTER 6

We had no choice but to keep on living.

Father's death changed us all. It was not only the black clothes that we all wore, the black that drew the color from Mirjana's soft pink cheeks and made my mother appear suddenly old. It was not only that we had to take care of the Inn by ourselves, manage the orchard and truck garden which was our second source of income, and somehow take care of the many tasks that he alone handled before. We did not complain of work. But Father was no longer there and we could not get used to the emptiness made by his absence.

Mama went about the house and the Inn, her face pale and her gaze distant as though she were not quite with us but existed somewhere else. Too busy to grieve openly during the day, she put aside her sorrows for night. She wept quietly then and once I heard her ask the same question over and over, "Why Milo? Why him? Why?" This question could not be answered.

"Do you hear Mama weeping when she's in bed?" I asked Mirjana one day as we were out collecting eggs from the hens.

"Yes," Mirjana replied. "But it's good that she's able to

cry. Don't say anything. If she held back all that grief and suffering, it would build up and break out in a violent way, like a dam bursting."

The amazing thing about my quiet sister was that she could sometimes be so wise. When my mother wept at night, I listened but knew better than to beg her to stop or to tell her it was no use. Sometimes it is best to let the tears flow.

Taking on my father's work changed all of us. Now on market days it was my mother and Marko who filled the truck with eggs, vegetables and baskets of fruit, while Mirjana and I managed the Inn. We were grateful that the tour buses still came, and often Mama had to take papa's place in welcoming visitors. But it was not the same without my father's genial manner which made everyone feel at home.

The food was still superb, of that we were certain, and the service was good. If we ran an inn in another place, we would do well, I thought, but here father's personality was stamped everywhere and we could not get used to his absence.

As time went on, Mama wept less. Either she was growing accustomed to our new life or else the minute her head touched the pillow, she fell asleep. But one day Mirjana and I compared notes and I found that she too thought Mama was changing. She was becoming stronger, even taller, so it seemed and when she said anything there was a certainty in her voice that had not been there before. She had always seemed to me like a quiet brown pheasant hen compared to my father's brilliant manner of the proud pheasant cock. Now she did not imitate him so much as she grew forceful and decisive in her own right.

One day when she was going to market, Mirjana asked

her a question about the menu; did we have enough lamb for *djuvec,* a kind of meat dish we sometimes made. At one time Mama would have said, "Don't ask me; your father will know," but on that day she considered the question and gave Mirjana a clear decisive answer. She tied the last ropes that held the produce on the truck, announced she would be back that afternoon and waved good-bye to us, as strong and determined as my father.

When it came time to go back to school, Mirjana said, "I've only a little more to go. Let me stay home and help you, Mamo."

"No, not at all," Mama said firmly. "You must not cheat your education. That is the most important thing."

Marko had hoped to get out of so much school, but Mama would have none of that either. We all got up earlier, worked harder, went to school, and worked more when we got home. There was no point in complaining; if we did not work, there would be nothing to eat.

One night when we were through cleaning the restaurant and the doors were locked, Mama said she wanted to talk with us. We sat around the heavy wooden table and sipped hot tea while she spoke.

"You can stop wearing black now. No more black. Tonight as I watched the two of you, all I could think of was how your father would have hated all that blackness. 'Enough, enough! I want my daughters to look pretty!' So from now on, you can put away those dark things and wear something with color, something pretty."

"*Hlava!* Thank you, Mamo!" I cried, jumping up and kissing her. Like my father, I detested this black dress I wore, as though I *needed* to wear it in order to remember him.

"What about you, Mamo? Will you change too?" Mirjana asked.

"For me it takes longer," she said. "Someday. In a while."

Mirjana and I did not have to be coaxed to get back to our other clothes.

We still mourned Father, but from time to time I noticed a secret smile on Mirjana's face.

"What's that all about, that smile?"

"I don't know what you're talking about," she said with pretended innocence.

Her secret was hardly well kept. More often now than ever before, the good-looking Mirko dropped in to visit us, to ask Mama if he could help in the orchards or with the livestock, but it was Mirjana he came to see, bringing her presents such as a whole wheel of cheese or a silk scarf he bought in Zagreb. Mama was pleased that he cared for Mirjana, but it would be some time before the two of them could announce whatever serious plans they may have been considering, because our family still mourned for Father.

Marko, now nine years old, was growing up. Not only did he have his usual chores, but he insisted on "doing things" like fixing the latticework on the terrace or rebuilding that part of the henhouse that had fallen down.

"Go out and play. You're still a little boy!" Mama said to him more than once.

"I'm the man of the house," he boasted, liking the sound of the phrase.

One day when he repeated this, I happened to be making bread and I broke off a bit of dough and threw it at him. "Man of the house, ho, ho, ho! When there are women like us, we don't need a man. Go ahead. You're still a 'little boy.' Do something important; go play baseball."

It was not easy to hurt his feelings or puncture his ego.

He placed his tongue between his lips and made a vulgar insulting sound. Had my father been here, what a scolding Marko would have had to endure!

"Why doesn't Mama ever say, 'Danica, you shouldn't have to work so hard; poor darling, you're only thirteen! Go over to Tanja's and pick daisies. Tell Tanja to come here and listen to the radio. Sing all the songs you like, Roberta Flaccus or Helen Reddy-made . . . anyone you like. I want to hear you giggling with Tanja, not see you drudging away your life in the kitchen!'"

"Poor little thing," Mirjana said sarcastically. She worked harder than I did and never complained. There was always work, and then more work, and when that was done, still more. And it was work I didn't like very much, floors to be scrubbed, dishes to be washed, clothes to be ironed, and of course, work in the Inn was never finished. How could Mirjana look forward to life on a farm, even a well-to-do farm where she would spend hours preparing meals that would be eaten in half an hour and the next day it would begin all over again. No matter how often you washed the dishes, more were waiting to be done; always clothes to be scrubbed; always the house to be dusted and put in order.

"But that's what life is, Danica," Mirjana said, "and if you love somebody, then you are glad to do it."

"Not for me!" I insisted, having scrubbed the last carrot for a stew; a basket of parsnips lay waiting to be sliced; after that the potatoes. When I became a doctor I would scrub my hands, but never again a carrot, a parsnip, a potato. Never.

Nobody knew of my decision to become a doctor, not even Tanja. If my mother knew, it would have upset her: "Not for you, Danica. We are plain people, simple people. Better to be like Mirjana and find yourself a husband." Worse yet, she would have become philosophical: "Well, you're young. We all have fancy ideas when we are thirteen. You'll get over them."

Mirjana would have echoed her thoughts. Tanja would flutter on about how wonderful I would look in a doctor's white coat if I told her.

I could not even tell Vesna, but when I went to see her one day, she welcomed me almost as if I were her daughter. I sat inside her hut, warming myself in front of her black iron stove, for it was beginning to get chilly outside, and after much talk, I asked her if she would teach me what she knew about herbs, midwifery, setting bones, curing fevers and anything else.

"You really *do* want to learn! If you will work, you can come and I will teach. Next summer you can be my assistant, would you like that?"

"Yes, yes!" I cried, filled with enthusiasm even though I knew the Inn would be there to take up my days.

"Splendid!" said Vesna. "You will be my protégé, that is, the one I teach, the one who will take my place when I am gone. What I teach you, you will not learn at the University in Zagreb, but still you must go to Medical School too. Then you will have many skills. Ah, that is good, that is splendid!"

Her enthusiasm made me so hopeful that I hugged her, although she is not particularly embraceable. At last it seemed as if I were going to do something worthwhile. For the first time since my father's death, I knew what it was to hope.

CHAPTER 7

Ever since my father's death, letters poured in from Uncle Ivo and Aunt Nevenka. They begged us to move to Vancouver, swore that the work of running the truck garden and the Inn would ruin our health, that the children would get a better education there, and so on and so on. Uncle Ivo even went so far as to make plans for my mother, but at least he did her the courtesy of telling her about them. She should sell everything she owned, he advised, and move to Vancouver where he would help her buy a place that she would turn into a first-class genuine Croatian restaurant. It would do well, it would flourish, in no time at all we would become rich, his letters implied. Vancouver was full of Croatians, he said, and not only they but all the non-Croatians would adore my mother's cooking.

"H'm" Mother said every time another letter came, as she put it in a basket with the rest of their letters. "Your father would not want us to leave Kalovar. We will manage."

"He would want us happy and comfortable, whatever would be best for us," I said in a very soft voice, for if I came on forcefully, she would only become more obdurate. Slowly I began to sense a weakness in her determination to stay.

Everything was beginning to go wrong with our life in Kalovar. One night, long before it was expected, a frost came, shriveling the tomatoes, killing our lettuces and other crops, and freezing all the growing produce that would have taken care of us that winter. We looked at each other with despair, Mirjana, Mama, even Marko, and I. Only a few green tomatoes were untouched, and these Mama picked and put on the windowsill to ripen.

Nor was that the last of our woes. A new road had been built five miles away, a road that the tour buses would henceforth take, and a new restaurant had been built to take care of the traffic, so that meant we would have to depend on the local villages for our income.

The tax bill came, greater than ever before. "How can I pay it?" Mama asked, worry lines furrowing her forehead.

One of the best goats died suddenly for no reason that we could discover.

And part of the roof blew off during a heavy storm. Mama and Marko tried to fix it, but this proved too much, and in the end they had to ask someone to do it for us.

"Everything seems to happen at once," Mirjana said.

"And maybe everything will get better all at once too," Mama said in an effort to cheer us, but she sounded so unhappy that we had to repeat what she said and insist that everything would get better. God would see to it.

Winter came early. Snows made the landscape a white vastness, hill folding into hill, broken only by the black of tree trunks and the patterns of black branches under a frosting of white. Only the black crows disturbed the pristine silence. Sometimes I wore my father's *kožuk,* a sheepskin jacket trimmed with red and black appliqués, but warm as it was, still I thought I would freeze.

Mama stayed in the house, weaving constantly at her loom, making a pile of place mats and coverlets. Early each spring someone came from Zagreb to buy handwork to sell in stores. She made very little compared to the prices that were charged there, "but we haven't much to say about it," she said sadly.

How I longed to say to her, "All we have to do is move to Vancouver." If only I dared to whisper the one word in her ear, "Vancouver!" but I knew the desire had to come from her.

One day she asked an apparently innocent question, making sure that Mirjana wasn't around. "Is it difficult to learn English, Danica?" This was my best subject and of course Mirjana had studied a little as well, with our teacher who had figured it out from reading a textbook.

"It's easy, Mamo, nothing to it," I assured her. "Instead of saying *Sdravo* you say 'Hello' or 'Good-bye.' "

"Doesn't sound hard. Hello? Good-bye?"

I wanted to hug her but restrained myself with a smile. The thought of Vancouver was beginning to grow in my mother, taking its time, like bread dough fermenting on a cool day, slowly but surely. From time to time I used the few English words I knew: *Good morning, Mother, dear. Thank you, Mother. Did you sleep well last night, Mother, dear?*

"What's that?" she would ask in Croatian, and sometimes she would repeat it, laughing at herself when she called herself "Mother, dear." "I would make so many mistakes," she laughed.

Still, I studied as hard as I could and made a point of teaching Marko so that "we could have a secret language."

46

As we did the dishes or collected eggs from the henhouse, we talked in English.

Only Mirjana was displeased. "I know exactly what you're trying to do. You want us to move. You think you're pretty sly, don't you?" she accused me, eyes flashing. "You know very well what Papa thought about our leaving home."

This time Mama did not agree with Mirjana, nor did she frown or ask why Marko and I talked English so much. The Inn had so few guests, she asked us one night, "Shall we close it entirely? We can open again in the spring."

Sadly enough we agreed it would be best. It was no comfort to us that everyone else in the villages had received notice of higher taxes. "Even the best-meaning friends can hardly afford to come," Mama said. We bolted the door of the Inn.

Another bill came in January. It was this, rather than grief for my father, that made my mother more desperate than I'd ever seen her. She sat at the kitchen table, eyes staring straight ahead, while outside in the freezing night, the snow drifted around the doors and windowpanes as if to shut us in forever. The wind never stopped howling. We may have heard wolves as well, or perhaps it was only the undying wind.

After a dinner of bleak cabbage soup, as I sat at the table to do homework and Mirjana knit a sweater and Marko played with a very pregnant cat, my mother sat alone at the table and did nothing. That worried me, that she was not knitting or weaving, reading, mending something or making plans for the spring garden. The latest tax bill lay on the table.

Finally she spoke. "Listen, children, the time has come. Mirjana put on a kettle of water. It's easier to talk over a

47

cup of hot tea. We have decisions to make."

She would not say any more until the tea was ready and we sipped the hot liquid, exchanging glances at the same time. Mama was up to something.

"You all know what this bill says. I don't know what to do any more. We cannot pay it."

Nobody said anything. We looked into our teacups as though the answer lay there. Mama went on.

"It will get worse, not better. I have been trying and trying and trying to find a solution, but what it is I don't know. Only one answer makes sense, but I could be wrong. What would you think about going to Canada?"

Marko's face lit up as though a hundred electric lights just turned on.

"Oh boy! Canada! I'll play hockey. I'll ski. I'll go sailing."

I smiled behind my hand, pleased that I prepared Marko so well, teaching him the right words for those things he loved most. An enormous hooray wanted to well out of me, but I knew better than to let it happen yet. I sighed as though the thought were painful.

"We don't have much choice, do we, Mamo? Not if they put us in jail for not paying taxes. It's not a bad solution."

Only Mirjana put down her knitting and tightened her lips, looking at each of us in disgust. Of course she wanted to stay in Croatia and marry Mirko. Mama, understanding this, patted her hand in sympathy.

"Poor Mirjana! I think of you too. I weigh your desires as well as your father's insistence that we stay here in Kalovar where we have always lived. But he would not want us to suffer. He would not like seeing the Inn empty either without much hope of its filling up again. He wouldn't want us to starve."

"But Mamo, you've spent your whole life here. How can you leave your home and all your friends? You've been through hard times before and you've come out all right," Mirjana pleaded, almost in tears.

"Where is there a law that says we must not go and find a better place?" Mama replied simply.

"And Uncle Ivo wants to help. He said he'd send us plane tickets," I said to support Mama.

Marko was already pretending to ski, play baseball and drive a fast car. I wanted to sing, and though Mama looked uncertain, she also had the appearance of someone who finds an impossible situation is not hopeless after all. Only Mirjana argued, begged us not to leave, promised everything would get better. But when she saw that Mama was serious about leaving, she gave in. "All right, I'll go too, but only long enough to help you get settled and begin your restaurant. And then I'm coming back. Kalovar is my home, the place I love."

Not Kalovar but Mirko, I was thinking. Had he not yet asked her to marry him then? "If you all want to go, then I'll go too," Mirjana said mournfully, and I hugged her for it. It was really going to happen, we were really going to go! I could hardly wait to tell Tanja in the morning, if I could make my way through the snow.

"All right," Mama said, neither happy nor depressed but somehow relieved as if this burden at least had been lightened. "We must remember to have faith and trust in God because what we are about to do will not be easy. We must remember always that we are Croatians and that we will always carry this knowledge in our hearts, within us. You know what I mean?"

Without thinking she put her hand on her heart as if to show that Croatia could rest there secure. She put her other arm around Mirjana to give her courage but could not reach Marko and me because we were dancing around like two happy lunatics.

"And tonight," Mama said, looking happier now, "we'll celebrate with some of our best *šljivovica*. At other times the best is for guests, but tonight we shall enjoy it!"

"*Zivalee!* Bravo!" Marko cried, as Mama unlocked the oak cupboard and brought out a bottle of our best plum brandy. That meant she was really serious about Canada. She filled our wineglasses and we touched them and held them high as we sang out our toasts.

"To Vancouver!" I cried.

"To hockey and swimming and skiing!" Marko yelled.

"To all of us!" Mirjana said, her voice unsure and faltering, yet brave.

But my mother's toast was the best of all. Her eyes were shining now as she lifted her glass. For a second we heard the wind outside battering at the door. Then she sang out her toast.

"To life! To a new and blessed life for all of us!"

We each touched our glasses to hers and then drank the rich, sweet brandy that came from our land.

CHAPTER 8

Once we had written Uncle Ivo of our decision to move to the New World, he made plans for us. In his letter he wrote, "It wasn't easy, believe me, Nadja, but I found a job for you as a cook in a good restaurant, so that you can begin to earn money right away. Then, when you speak English good and get used to Canada, we shall open a Croatian restaurant, you and I."

" 'Speak English *good'*?" I questioned. "He should maybe speak better." At least I had been studying my grammar.

But my mother's eyes became luminous with every new promise. She was becoming more and more enthusiastic about beginning a new life.

"What's more," Uncle Ivo wrote, "I have accomplished another miracle. I found a place for you to live, a suite of rooms in the Villa Rosanna in the West End, which is one of the most elegant parts of the city."

"Villa Rosanna! Villa Rosanna! It sounds too good to be true," I said, dreaming of a country house with lawns, gardens and fountains. That is what the word *villa* conjured up in my mind.

"Don't get your hopes up too high," my mother said

with realistic expectations; she knew we would probably not be living in a palace there. The idea of a villa made no difference to Mirjana, who still did not want to leave and only shook her head as though it did not concern her.

But Tanja was as excited as if she were going with us. We found a picture of a villa in a book at school, a long, low, sprawling house with stables in back, a gazebo, a long row of cypress trees, a small lake and formal gardens with wide marble stairs and fountains.

"Not bad," I cried.

But Tanja, looking through my postcards and pamphlets Uncle Ivo had sent, pointed out that the West End he talked about was filled with apartment houses sometimes referred to as the high-rising towers. "But I wouldn't mind living in a tower," I told Tanja, "such as this one here. We would live on the top floor and see for miles around."

I could not tell which vision appealed to me more, the low-lying villa or the penthouse, visions which couldn't be resolved into one image but it didn't matter. Either of them would do.

I became more of a dreamer than ever.

Preparing to leave Kalovar was a more real experience, and my dreams floated away in a mist as we were suddenly faced with decisions that never before occurred to us. Mama sat at the kitchen table at the end of the day and sometimes she sighed in such a way that I knew this move was not going to be easy. "Please, God, don't let her change her mind," I prayed.

Mirjana didn't make it any easier and quietly she argued with Mama, urging her not to leave. "There will never be plums like the plums we grow in our orchard. Will you find peaches like ours in that northern country? And grapes, Mamo, think of our grapes, the same vines that you transplated from your own home here. How can you give them up?"

Then she talked about the fig tree. Mama had transplanted it after a visit to a cousin who lived near the Dalmatian coast. Everyone told her it was too cold in Kalovar for a fig tree, but she found a sheltered place for it and though it did not grow, still it survived. She cared for that tree as a mother cares most for a poor, stunted child. Mirjana hit a sensitive spot when she said, "Mamo, how can you leave it behind?"

"But we're not trees. We'll transplant all right," I argued. "Others have."

Had we realized how much we had to leave behind, however, we might have decided to stay in Kalovar after all. We could not take the trees we had loved and cared for all our lives. The animals would have to stay behind, my darling Snowball and the other goats, the cows, my mother's chickens, even the half-wild cats that stayed with us.

"What will happen to my goats!" Tears rolled down my cheeks as I milked Snowball, who turned and stared at me with her glassy eyes, not understanding this strange emotion. Would I have to take her to market? If so, then surely someone might butcher her.

"I won't let that happen, I won't," I promised Snowball, who at this point nibbled indifferently at a thistle head and undoubtedly thought I was simply peculiar, like most human beings.

But I kept my promise to her by persuading Tanja to beg her father to buy all five goats. She promised him she would take care of them and assured me they would never be slaughtered. What's more, we were allowed to keep them until the day we left.

That was only one problem. For the first time in our lives we realized we had many possessions, good Croatian-made pottery that my father sometimes bought on market days, our sheepskin jackets with their designs in appliqué leather, brass pots such as we might never find again, the solid carved chairs and heavy decorative chests and my mother's loom. We had used these things, grown up with them and become so used to them that they seemed part of us. Such things could never be replaced. "Would they have strong oak tables in Canada, as ancient and sound as our kitchen table? And what about the hand-carved bed Papa and I have slept in all these years. How can I leave that behind?" Mama asked.

It was clear we couldn't carry this table or that bed on the plane with us. We were allowed only so many pounds and so we constantly made decisions about what we would take and then changed our mind.

"Guess what," Marko cried. "You can take dogs in a special cage, so we can take Stanko with us!"

"In Canada you can find dogs, of that I'm positive," Mama said.

"But not like Stanko! He's a good shepherd!" Marko cried, tears in his voice.

"I know how you feel," I sympathized. "I have to leave my goats. Or else I'd take Snowball."

"Look here," Mama said with unexpected strength. "I'm getting tired of all this weeping and worrying. If we are going to have a new life, then we have to leave the old behind; we cannot take it *all* with us. So each one will choose one thing—not an animal, that's an extra fare—so choose what means most to you. And if there's room for anything more, we'll take it. We'll use every last ounce of weight we're allowed."

That was the end of the argument. Once again I was surprised to find she was becoming very strong and spoke decisively, as my father would have spoken.

It was easy for me to make my choice, the wooden chest

my father had given me, a pretty chest with birds and flowers carved and painted all over it. "It's funny," I confided in Tanja, "I used to feel hurt because Mirjana's chest was so much bigger than mine. Now hers is too big and heavy to take, but mine is just right. Poor Mirjana, she has to leave hers behind."

Aunt Nevenka wrote to us, advising that we take our best costumes with us, all the embroidered blouses, skirts, aprons, kerchiefs and woven cloths that we had, for those we would not find easy to replace. We could easily buy everyday clothes in Vancouver. So we packed our voluminous skirts and blouses, slipping among them photographs, what jewelry we owned, my father's tambourica and everything else we could slip in.

Mama took us to the dressmaker and had new clothes made for us, so that we would not feel ashamed when our relatives met us. When I looked in the mirror at my new navy blue skirt, my white shirt and heavy brown coat, I stood tall and pleased with myself. "I'm beginning to look Canadian already," I thought.

The people who bought the house and the Inn also bought much of the heavy furniture, so we did not suffer the pain of seeing it moved out. But the floor looked sadly bare where we had to take up the rug when we sold it, and as the other objects disappeared, my mother's loom and Mirjana's beautiful wooden chest and even the cradle that was still brightly painted although we had not used it for years, the house seemed abandoned. One afternoon I saw the tears in Mama's eyes that rose at the empty look of the room. "I just feel bad about it," she confessed. I began to cry too. Then we hugged each other and she said, "We must make a beautiful new home. We must look ahead or else we will drown in regrets." Then we wiped our eyes, blew our noses and went on with the packing.

CHAPTER 9

During that last month before we left, I learned that the people of Kalovar not only seemed to care for us, but that they were overflowing with endless good advice.

The schoolmaster drilled me in English and more than once talked to me after school. "You must learn to speak English perfectly; you must study very hard in all subjects; and you must go to college because you have a good mind. Someday," he prophesied, "all Kalovar will be proud of you!" I liked the flattery; I agreed with him though nobody could have been more ignorant than I.

Jure also had good advice. "You musn't become like city girls. It will be bad for you. It will ruin you. You will not be the same."

Then he became downcast as we walked along the road. "What's wrong with becoming a city girl?" I asked.

"You will forget me. You will forget Kalovar. I will never see you again."

"Poor Jure!" I comforted him although again I was flattered by his attention. "Then you can come over there and find me."

"Not me, Danica. I will stay here."

He said this with conviction, and as I looked into his

sincere brown eyes, I felt sad to be leaving my friend.

I saw little of Vesna during my last months. My head was filled with Canada and the great trip that lay ahead. I even forgot that I was to become her student once school was over and I had time to go with her to gather herbs and accompany her when she went to deliver babies and treat sick people and animals.

One afternoon she waited for me in the schoolyard. She beckoned me with a crook of her forefinger. Many children feared her and wondered that I was so glad to see her again.

"I hear you are going far away," she said.

"Yes, to Canada." I could not hide my enthusiasm. She nodded as though accepting a fate that could not be altered.

"I see. Yes. I was afraid of that. I had hoped you would become my successor. I am getting old and somebody should be able to take my place. You were the one destined for this."

"I'm really sorry. I looked forward to studying with you."

"I would not take on just anyone, you know," she said, holding me with her unwavering gaze. "You have the gift to heal. It is a sin to abuse God's gift, to let it go to waste, to forget it."

"Vesna, I will not forget it. I can study medicine in Canada and become a doctor there. And I will never forget you."

She put her old gnarled hand over mine, then surprised me by hugging me, and I embraced her too.

"God bless you!" she said at last, then turned and waddled off down the road toward her hut.

The surprise party the villagers planned for us was hardly a surprise. As the day grew near, Tanja's eyes grew big as she said, "Wait and see! It's going to be a big party. Just wait!"

We were overwhelmed. Mama had thought perhaps a few close friends would have a small party for us; after all, it had always been Papa who was the well-known figure of the family. But the night before we were to leave it seemed as if everyone in Kalovar came out dressed in their best and bringing food and wine for a real feast. The party was held where all celebrations were held, at the Inn; We were not allowed to serve food or cook or wash dishes, but were treated like royal guests. Musicians came too, with *tambouras, tambouricas,* violins, accordions and guitars.

There were speeches, some of them long and flowery, mountains of food, many embraces and then the dancing, the best part of all! We joined hands and danced in circles, first one way, then the other. Everyone danced from little children to the oldest grandfathers and grandmothers. As the dances became faster and more intricate, the older people and the children dropped out, but I kept dancing, twirling, kicking, always moving to the music as though I had a devil inside of me that would not let me stop. Mirjana and Mirko were the best dancers of all, and more than once the rest of us stood around, applauded and shouted the familiar cries and whistles as those two performed alone.

"The Festivals won't be the same without you," people told Mirjana over and over. Suddenly a great throb of sorrow welled up in me. I would never dance at Zagreb now. Naturally Mirjana and I did not perform that last summer when we mourned for Papa, though I was glad when Tanja took my place. Now I would never dance at Zagreb; it was a big price to pay. Here we were, ready to leave, and for the first time I wished we were staying after all.

Then Jure came over and asked me to be his partner in the next *kolo*. We danced and I knew I would miss him too. Mama was busy with her friends and yet she watched to see that we did not drink too much *šljivovica*. When we were tired dancing, we all sat around and began to sing. What a long party, what a great party, what a wonderful feeling that we were all together! It was six in the morning when the last song was sung. Some of the guests got up, yawned loudly and went to milk their cows and begin the new day without having slept at all. Mama made us go to bed. Marko had already fallen asleep, but Mirjana's eyes were wide and I was too excited to sleep.

Tomorrow we would be leaving Kalovar, perhaps forever.

The day after the party we stood by the side of the road, waiting for the bus to pick us up and take us to Zagreb where we would take another bus to the airport. Mama checked again and again to make sure she had the tickets Uncle Ivo sent us. We did not look quite familiar to one another in our new clothes, nor could we quite believe we were actually on our way.

Although everyone had said good-bye to us at the party, still people came to see us off. They brought gifts, a home-cured ham, a jar of honey, bottles of plum brandy, elaborate coffee cakes and aged cheeses, and an intricately plaited basket to hold all these foods. Mama's eyes grew misty at all these reminders of our home.

Tanja, sniffling, smiling and clinging to me by turns, gave me a shawl she herself had woven and a kerchief she had embroidered with flowers and a message in red thread that wound between the bright colored blossoms. "Don't forget me, don't forget me, don't forget me!"

"I won't, Tanja," I cried, hugging her. "I'll never find another friend like you. Never!"

"You all look different already and you haven't even left," a woman remarked to my mother, proud in her new suit that the dressmaker said was "the latest thing." She carried a new purse under her arm as well, a city purse instead of the old woven bag she always used at home.

Marko capered around like a happy monkey, but it was a difficult time for Mirjana. She and Mirko had eyes only for each other, eyes that filled with tears as they clung to one another. Even when the bus came along, stopping with a hiss and a shudder, and we all got on, Mirjana and Mirko were still embracing, calling each other pet names and promising to wait for one another. The driver grew impatient and tooted his horn. "Hey, Miss, are you going to get on this bus or not?" The older women sighed sympathetically at this sad parting, but the children were imitating them in an unkind way.

I felt sorry for Mirjana. For her, parting from Mirko was as tragic and romantic as a scene in an opera and not unlike some of the sad folk songs about doomed lovers, but I had to confess that she looked silly as strands of hair tumbled down from her finely twisted chignon, her nose grew red and moist and she had to blow it frequently, and her eyes were pink and wet with tears. Reluctantly she climbed on the bus.

All the good people of Kalovar, our neighbors, the good friends we knew all our lives, wished us a good journey, begged us to write to them and above all, to remember them.

"Remember Kalovar! Do not forget us!" they cried.

They waved to us as the bus pulled out, and we leaned out of the window and waved our handkerchiefs back to them, our eyes never leaving them until the bus came to a curve and then bumped down the dusty road. Then we could not see our friends or Kalovar any more.

CHAPTER 10

How can I describe what it is like to fly for the first time? Aren't you frightened, Tanja had asked me, and I had answered, of course not. Yet as we waited at Zagreb Airport, my stomach seemed to be rising and falling, and I kept having to go to the Ladies' Room.

"You look pale, little one," Mama said sympathetically. But I couldn't have looked more white than she or Mirjana. The two of them closed their eyes from time to time and moved their lips, praying, I suppose. Mirjana's face mirrored tragedy as though she had just suffered a great loss, and Mama's fears were practically written on her face: What if she should be punished for leaving Kalovar against her husband's wishes? What if the plane blew up or crashed into another plane? What if it fell into the ocean and her children drowned? She would be the one to blame.

Only Marko took everything in stride as he ran about the airport in a frantic effort to see everything, giving my mother a new worry, that the plane would take off without him.

"Stop worrying, Mamo. There's nothing to be afraid of. Hundreds of planes fly all the time without accidents. Marko won't get lost."

The words were brave but my stomach betrayed me and I had to rush off to the Ladies' Room once more.

Finally we were settled on the plane, but by then Mama had new worries. Did we have the tickets, could we be sure the luggage was on the right plane (the men who handled the baggage appeared so *casual*), could the pilot see well enough to fly in the dark of night without getting lost? Fastening the seat belt assured her we were going to the moon!

At last the motors roared. The plane circled around the field, paused, and then with one determined growl rushed across the field and up into the sky. It was an ecstasy like nothing I'd ever experienced in all my life. We were flying! We were flying! I began to laugh with the wonder of it, and my fears vanished.

Marko grinned at me, his eyes shining.

"*Zivalee!*" he said. Bravo! He was as excited as I, but Mama and Mirjana clutched each other, both of them terrified.

"Look down there!" I cried. "That's Zagreb!"

Somehow they found the courage to look down at the city, all lit up and twinkling in the night, but no sooner did they look than we were already passing it. The hills and fields were dark, but now and then we saw clusters of lights as we passed over small towns and villages. Up ahead were the high, dark mountains of the north. I would never have believed we could leave our country so fast.

"Good-bye, Croatia," I whispered, lest the other passengers hear me. Yet I wanted to say good-bye. Kalovar was down there, a dark little village in the deep purple night. Suddenly I thought of Snowball, of Tanja, of the pine grove, the carved bed under the eaves where I would never sleep again, and the tears came to my eyes. The fields of wheat would come up in the spring with the new green blades piercing the soil, and I would not be there to see them. Nor would I hear the women sing at harvest time when the wheat was gathered and tied in shocks. I would not see our orchards burst into bloom. Never again would I go to the village school.

For the first time I realized what was meant by the term "the mother country." Croatia was my mother, with its fields and villages; I came from its soil, I was nourished by it, and now I was leaving it, leaving the warm familiar homeland to go where I'd never been before. Painful, it was painful!

Good-bye, Croatia, motherland.

We had to wait at the airport outside Amsterdam. "Two hours, Mamo! Let's go out and look at the canals and the palace!"

"No, Danica. The man told us we have to stay here. If we get lost, we'll never get to Vancouver," Mama said, still tense with worry.

"Anyway," Mirjana said, having recovered from emotional shock and becoming her sensible self once more, "the airport is miles from the city and we'd have to go through customs and all that. Not a chance of it."

It seemed a pity to be so close to this old city and not be able to see it. Yet the airport itself was brimming with people who spoke French, Dutch, Italian, Japanese and other languages I could not recognize. Who were these people? Where were they going?

"Stop staring. It isn't nice," Mirjana said.

But who could stop staring when everyone seemed so stylish and self-assured. A woman in a sleek fur coat sauntered by with a poodle on a leash; that dog's collar sparkled with gems as if he were royalty. In comparison we felt more countrified and awkward each time a chic woman or well-tailored man swept across the floor in front of us.

"We look like peasants," I grumbled. "We look terrible!"

Mama shook her head and looked hurt, so instead of criticizing the new clothes which had cost so much, I vented my disappointment on the innocent basket full of delicacies that our friends had given us. "Traveling with all that makes us look stupid, as if we didn't know they would feed us on the plane."

"*Uzdaj se u se i u svoje kljuse,*" my mother said, and this old Croatian proverb which my father often quoted put me in my place. It means, "Have pride in yourself and in your horse. Even if you are poor, don't be ashamed."

Mama held her head high, but our reflection in a glass door told me that we did look like bumpkins. The new clothes which were "the latest thing" in Kalovar suddenly became bulky, dull and tasteless. Marko, with his small knit cap looked as if he ought to be out herding the sheep, not riding Air Canada. But I looked the worst of all with that brown coat that was too short and my skirt that was too long and ugly clumpy shoes.

Never mind, I comforted myself, as soon as I got to Vancouver I would go to a store and buy clothes that were already made. In Canada I would become as beautiful as a girl with long hair who moved slowly across the waiting room; I would wear a skirt like hers, a long, fitted coat and a silk scarf that seemed to float in the air behind her as she walked by.

"Come," said Mama. "Time to go."

We all had hand luggage to carry. With a marked lack of graciousness, I picked up the offending basket of food and followed her.

The plane was late in starting, so we went without sleep for many hours and did not get to Vancouver until nearly midnight. Mama's eyes still reflected a fundamental distrust. "It's not natural for people to fly," she said, then compressed her lips with fear.

Mirjana became more of a worrier than ever, asking in that last part of the journey, "What if Uncle Ivo is not there to meet us, what will we do, where can we go?" She began to figure out plans of action we could take until Mama, who was always so gentle, burst out with one word, "Quiet!" so unexpectedly loud that a few passengers turned around to stare at her. Now she was embarrassed as well as nervous.

"There it is!" someone cried. We peered out of the windows and looked down to see Vancouver, a vast place sparkling with lights, red, yellow and white, a city that twinkled proudly in the middle of a dark enormity of night country and the ocean. The plane descended slowly through the air.

Beautiful Vancouver! I loved it already. Our new home! Our new land!

CHAPTER 11

Mama mumbled a prayer of thanks and then sighed with relief as the plane came to a stop and the stewardess thanked us for riding Air Canada. Dizzy with excitement and lack of sleep, we followed the other passengers to the airport, Mama almost at wit's ends because Marko was doing cartwheels all the way down the red carpet.

Before we could see Aunt Nevenka and Unclo Ivo, we had to go through customs, which meant waiting in line while suitcases, boxes and bags were opened and examined by officials. Everything was checked with an "all right" or an "okay" until Mama placed the large basket with its hams, cheeses and preserves on the counter. The official shook his head sadly as he took out the food.

"What are you doing?" Mama asked, perplexed.

No translator was around, but I knew enough English to catch the drift of what he was saying. We were not allowed to bring food into Canada, because of the laws.

"It's good food," Mama tried to explain, unable to understand why the official gave us back the basket with only the two bottles of brandy we were allowed. "Maybe he's hungry?" she asked me.

"No, Mamo," Mirjana explained. "There could be diseases or molds on the food. Something like that. It's a health regulation."

"It's good food," Mama repeated. Canada was already a puzzling country to her.

"I am very sorry," the official explained in a kind way, "but that is the law. I hope you will like Canada."

Mama was upset as she walked away, but then made the best of it. "If that's the worst thing that happens to us in this new country, it won't be so bad we won't survive."

Yet it was a sad end to the gifts given to us so generously. The friends who gave us the hams would have less meat because of us; the cheeses took time and skill to make; the preserves were made from berries that had to be gathered, then mixed with expensive sugar and probably boiled on a steaming hot summer day. They were gifts of love. Now I felt ashamed for having complained about carrying the basket.

But the basket was soon forgotten as we followed the crowds into the waiting room. At the last minute I too began to worry; what if the relatives weren't there to meet us, what if they didn't recognize us? For a moment we stood there, dazed, four country people with arms full of packages; and then we saw Uncle Ivo and Aunt Nevenka at the same time that they saw us. Hugging, kissing and embracing followed, with sudden tears and laughter and everyone talking at once!

"We're here, we made it! We didn't fall into the ocean after all!" Mama cried with relief. "And here you are to greet us. Look at you!"

Although I was too young when Aunt Nevenka and Uncle Ivo had left home to be able to recognize them now, it was clear that Canada must have been good to them. Uncle Ivo seemed to be wearing a small round pillow under his well-tailored coat, and the heaviness in his cheeks suggested he was well fed. Aunt Nevenka's fur coat looked lush and expensive, and her black hair, piled high on her head, made her seem a grand lady, not someone who once lived in Kalovar. But it was their daughter, my cousin Marija, twenty years old and lovely that I stared at. How she smiled, how like an actress she was with chestnut hair softly curled, a pale leather coat tied with a belt to show off her tiny waist, and creamy boots with high heels and laces pulled tight so that they fit snugly around her slender legs. I could not wait to become just like Marija, a real Canadian.

"So you're Danica," she said after her parents were finished kissing me and telling Mama what a handsome girl I was. However, I knew that relations cannot be trusted in such matters. They would have told her I was handsome if I had been born with two eyes on one side of my head and three running noses. It was only Marija's opinion that I wanted.

"You and Mirjana are so pretty! You'll have a wonderderful time in Canada. We'll have lots of fun together."

She spoke in Croatian, but she did not speak it correctly or easily.

"If you want to talk in English, is all right. I understand a little," I said, actually very proud, of course, but my pride lasted less than a minute.

"I'm sorry, what did you say? I don't speak Croatian very well," Marija said.

"I am now speaking English," I repeated. "English. Canadian. If you want to talk in English, is all right."

This time she caught the drift of what I was saying. "You must have learned English in Kalovar," she answered, smiling and turning to Mirjana.

It was clear even on this brief meeting that it was Mirjana who would become her friend. After all, Mirjana was seventeen, closer to her age than I, and yet I could not help but feel jealous when Marija walked with Mirjana out to the car. I stopped to glance at myself in the mirror, a quick glance to be sure, at a Danica whose face was white with lack of sleep, a jealous Danica who wished she could slip off the coat which now seemed uglier and thicker than ever compared to Marija's trim leather coat.

"Look at her," Mirjana said of me to Marija, who seemed to understand her very easily. "Impossible to pull her away from the mirror."

"If I looked that pretty, I'd stand in front of the mirror too," Aunt Nevenka said. She, at any rate, was on my side.

"She's a very pretty girl, Nadja," Uncle Ivo said to my mother. "You'll have a hard time keeping the boys away from her."

So now Mama had something new to worry about! I could read it in her face, but it was an encouraging thought. Would the boys really like me, I wondered. Would they be nice like Jure or would they tease like the others?

"Danica's a good, sensible girl. I can tell," Aunt Nevenka said.

"So far yes," my mother said, "but it is not easy to bring up children without a father."

She sighed and Uncle Ivo comforted her.

"You will do fine," he said. "You did the right thing to come here."

At last our baggage was collected and we were riding home in Uncle Ivo's long, bronze-colored station wagon. I could not believe the city was so big; it went on and on, over rivers and bays, with lights everywhere and a cluster of lights that seemed to linger in the sky.

"That's Grouse Mountain," Uncle Ivo explained. "Sometime we shall go there."

We must have crossed three bridges and gone through a tunnel or two, when suddenly I recognized that section of the city that had appeared on several of the postcards that Aunt Nevenka had sent us. Tower after tower, buildings over thirty stories high, with golden light streaming from the hundreds of squares that were windows, repeated itself in the shimmering reflections in the waters of English Bay. This was the West End where we would live!

"It's so beautiful! Even better than the postcards. What a wonderful place!" I cried, clasping my hands. It was a sight that still has magic for me, even after all the time that I've been here.

Marko loved it too; we hugged each other, making silly noises out of sheer delight.

"I'll live there," Marko cried, pointing to a tower that had spines of blue lights up and down its sides. "On the top floor!"

Uncle Ivo threw his head back and laughed while Aunt Nevenka and Marija smiled. "So you want to live in the Hydro-Electric Company, Marko? That would be something new; maybe they're looking for a bright new executive."

"Don't let Uncle Ivo tease you," Aunt Nevenka said. "Maybe you will be up there some day."

Mama was exchanging village gossip with Aunt Nevenka, and Marija and Mirjana were becoming fast and exclusive friends, so I showed off to Marko by reading advertising signs, all kinds of signs glittering in the night.

"Stop. Go. Walk."

"GAS. See, Marko, that's a gas station."

"Dummy, as if I didn't know."

"Su-per Valu?" I said doubtfully. Did they spell it right?

"It's a chain of supermarkets," Marija explained, which left me as confused as ever. I knew what a chain was, but a "chain of markets" and what was this, a "*super*-market"?

Uncle Ivo turned left, and while he stopped at a red light, I continued to read the signs, not realizing that at that particular moment everyone was quiet. Of all the signs on the street, I had to chose the worst one: "Strip-a-rama. Go-go dancers. Apply Fred!" I read the syllables without any idea of what that meant. In our English grammar in Kalovar, there were no such words.

Immediately our three relatives burst out laughing.

"I don't understand," I said, embarrassed at their hilarity. "What is this, a 'streep-a-rama'?"

"A good place for you to keep away from," Uncle Ivo said. "It's a show in a nightclub where girls strip off their clothes . . ."

Mama gasped with this new worry. "You mean girls take off their dresses?" I asked.

"Their dresses and lots more. Go-go dancing is not like the *kolo*," Aunt Nevenka said; the *kolo* is a dignified circle dance in Croatia and in Serbia too and the dancers are always well clothed.

"And don't trust Fred!" Marija laughed.

Fortunately for me, the subject changed when a loud siren assaulted us and a long red truck, an overpowering spectacle with red and yellow lights flashing and engine roaring, rushed past us up the street.

This time I had the sense to say nothing. Then Uncle

71

Ivo proudly explained about fire engines and what a splendid fire department we had in Vancouver, as if he had been responsible for directing all of it.

The traffic lights changed, and as Uncle Ivo drove us up one street and down another, Marko and I thought that any minute we'd see the Villa Rosanna. We tried to see the tops of the buildings, but they were too high. We were so excited we punched each other softly.

At last Uncle Ivo coasted down a street lined with trees and high apartment buildings, and then stopped in front of a squat three-story brick building, that looked old-fashioned compared to the two gleaming high-rise buildings on either side of it.

"Which one is ours?" Marko asked. "This one or that?" Like me he was certain we would live on the top story of one of the towers.

"Neither one, little darling," Aunt Nevenka said. "It is this lovely house in front of us with the magnolia tree. A good location too. You're only three blocks from the beach, from English Bay."

Marko and I understood each other's disappointment. But I liked the tree which seemed to be lit up with hundreds of waxy white blossoms. And if we lived in "a suite of rooms" on the third floor, surely it was higher than any building in Kalovar! We picked up our luggage and followed Uncle Ivo, only to be surprised again!

Instead of walking *up* to the third floor, we followed our uncle *down* a flight of steps to a basement apartment. He unlocked the door, turned on a switch with a flourish as though it would flood the place with light, and said, "Welcome to your new home!"

Our new home! In a city built of towers, we were going to live in a basement. In the dim light we could see that what windows we had were placed just under the ceiling and the magnificent views we had imagined before we came would most likely be the legs of people walking by.

"Do you like it?" Aunt Nevenka cooed, as though she expected us to sing Halleluja any minute. Why, even Kalovar was better than this. Mama glared at us, meaning we shouldn't say anything, no matter how bad we felt.

"Come, I'll show you the apartment, Nadja," Aunt Nevenka said as Uncle Ivo brought in the rest of our possessions, which made a pitiful heap of things in the middle of the floor.

"That was the living room, of course, and this is the kitchen," Aunt Nevenka announced.

"This little place?" Mama asked, the words uttered slowly. "A *kitchen?*" It was less than six feet square, too small for more than one person; in Kalovar the kitchen was bigger than this whole apartment, with its enormous black monster of a stove and enormous oak table and benches and chests.

"Now, Nadja," Aunt Nevenka scolded, "this is not a barn. See, here's a clean electric stove, no wood to chop, no fires to start. And I've brought you dishes and pans and groceries, to help you out until you're settled."

"You are very good to us. Thank you, Nevenka," Mama said, hugging her, but her eyes betrayed her. She was still horrified to think that this would be a kitchen, *her* kitchen.

There was a small bathroom, a bedroom for Mama and another small bedroom for Mirjana and me, all of them dark and unappealing. "And Marko?"

"He will sleep in the living room. The sofa folds into a bed. It's really so clever to have a sofa all day, a bed all night," Aunt Nevenka said.

Marko's jaw dropped in disappointment. At home my father had built a small balcony where he could sleep on hot summer nights; in the winter he had a corner of the loft where he kept all his treasures, a jar full of tadpoles, his baseball, his bat, an old accordion he was going to fix someday. Now he had no place at all.

"All right," Uncle Ivo said, as we could not hide our chagrin to think we had given up our spacious home in Kalovar for these stingy rooms. "It's not like home, but believe me, you are lucky to have a place to lay your head."

"Thank you. We are very lucky," Mama repeated woodenly.

"It is a good part of the city," Uncle Ivo went on. "You are only two blocks from work, the children will go to school; there is a big park nearby. Beautiful exclusive buildings where rich people live. Lucky for you, I got connections."

Mama jumped as a shrill whistle sounded from the kitchen. "What's that?"

"A tea kettle," Marija explained. "It whistles when the water boils. I boiled some water so we could all have tea. We brought over some cakes for you."

"And tomorrow you come to our house for dinner," Aunt Nevenka said.

As she set the table, suddenly I wanted to leave this stifling place and go outside.

"All right, but be careful, Danica," my uncle warned. "Remember, this is a big city and it's full of wolves waiting to eat up a girl like you. Don't go too far. You'll get lost."

It wasn't as if I were three years old, I grumbled, and I wasn't afraid either, I muttered under my breath as I went out into the chilly April night. The city was quiet, many of the windows dark now, for people had to go to bed here just as they did in Kalovar. I heard the dull roar of autos a few streets away, and sounds of laughter from a building that rose high and white into the dark sky. I noticed that the trees lining both sides of the street were still bare-limbed although they had already begun to blossom and leaf out at home. I'd never seen any tree like that blooming magnolia.

"At least I love that tree," I admitted, "and it belongs to us."

In the distance between the bulk of two high buildings, I saw a ripple of water shimmering in the night. I had never seen a large body of water before, but even that small glimpse of it filled me with an excitement that more than made up for the miserable little rooms that were to be our home. As I began to walk down the street toward the Bay, Aunt Nevenka called me back.

"Come, darling. It will still be there tomorrow morning. Come and have tea and cake. Then you can crawl into bed and sleep after your long trip."

Before I followed her back into the Villa, I caught a last glimpse of the gleaming water. Someday I would live high, high, high, as I had in my dreams, at the top of one of the magic towers, and I would be a true Canadian, as beautiful as Marija.

CHAPTER 12

In the morning we were jolted awake by what seemed to be a sudden torrent of heavy rain, alarmingly close, as if it were in the house. Mirjana jerked up in her bed at the same time I did, both of us wondering what was happening. Then we heard Mama scolding Marko. He was trying the shower without knowing anything about the way it worked. First it was cold so that he was pelted with needles of cold water. His screams called Mama from her bed.

"I'm freezing!" Marko yelled.

"Turn the handles the other way," Mama shouted over the sound of the water.

He obeyed and now clouds of steam were filling the tiny bathroom and spreading everywhere through the suite while Marko screamed. "I'm burning to death! I'm scalded!" My mother reached in, turned the faucets and shut off the water. The tiny bathroom was a disaster of water and steam, but Marko danced around with a towel around his waist as he grinned at us.

"Hey, try it. It's fun!"

"Fun? Then you can clean the bathroom," Mama said, not amused in the least. "Pay attention, all of you.

There's a curtain around the shower; first you pull it tight so the water doesn't go all over the floor. And don't turn it on so hard."

"You should have asked me," Mirjana said. "There are showers like this in Zagreb. I know how they work."

Marko made a funny face. Mirjana always knew everything! What a maddening person she could be!

We dressed. Mama looked around the suite in the dim morning light. "So this is Canada!" she said, sighing at this mean, gloomy place that would be our home. "Not what I expected, but we have to make the most of it."

She touched the clammy plastic-covered table in the living room, cried "Ech!" at its cold dampness and immediately rummaged through one of the suitcases and took out a handwoven tablecloth she had brought with us and placed it on the table. "There, that's better!"

I felt somewhat mixed up, for I had expected to love everything Canadian, and yet it was a relief to see the familiar tablecloth with its geometrical red border covering that ugly green tabletop.

"Very strange furniture," Mama said, frowning. "What is it, wood, metal? Not like anything I've ever seen." Nor did she like it either. Out of the suitcase came an embroidered cloth to cover the wobbly coffee table, and a square of linen to be pinned over the stained brownish covering of a stuffed chair.

Mama sighed and shuddered once more at the miserable living room. "The table we had at home was so old, nobody knew how old, and it was so solid three men could stand on it and dance."

"Mamo," Mirjana said in a warning voice. "Remember what you said, we mustn't look back."

"I'd forgotten already! You're right. Let's have only good thoughts, like how nice Aunt Nevenka was to get this furniture for us. She left food for us too. How about breakfast?''

Mama opened a breadbox and took out a rectangular loaf wrapped in a plastic bag and tied with a piece of plastic. "This is bread? Already sliced." She held up a slice of pure white bread. "It looks manufactured, as if it were not quite real. Reminds me of false teeth."

At the same time, Mirjana was rummaging through the refrigerator. She took out a cardboard carton filled with sticks of neatly wrapped butter, and a large plastic carton. She opened the spout and looked inside. "Milk? I think it's milk. Milk in a box. That's funny."

"Hey, I'm starving while you're exploring," Marko said.

"Of course, here, darling," Mama said as she tried to spread the hard butter over a slice of bread. Marko began to wolf it, then put it down.

"Hey, Mamo, it tastes funny. Are you sure it's bread? It's more like cotton."

Mama took a bite and made a face. "Tomorrow I'll buy yeast and flour, if you can find it in a place like this; and we'll make our own bread, like we had at home. Wish I could make our own butter too."

Mirjana took down from the cupboard a cardboard box decorated with pictures of children riding around in cars. "What's this?"

"Sugar pawps," I read slowly, "the cereal that tastes like candy."

"Ah, cereal. That's good," Mama said. "Try that, Marko. But why should it taste like candy?"

At home cereal was barley, wheat or farina, kept in wooden canisters rubbed smooth from generations of use. Here, we would have to get used to cardboard boxes and plastic containers. Mama opened the box, gave Marko a small yellow disc and bit into one herself.

"Tastes like cardboard," she said. "Maybe we're eating the box. They must have made a mistake in the factory. This can't be food."

"At least this has to be better," Mirjana said as she took out a box of eggs from the refrigerator. "The hen made the container, real shell, not cardboard or plastic."

By this time we were all starving, and Mama said at least eggs would nourish us as she set about melting butter in the pan and telling me to set the table so we could eat right away. I was getting more and more hungry and Mama didn't have to beg us to come to the table, for we were there, waiting. But when I poked my fork in the egg yolk, out came a thin pale yellow liquid. That did it! I could not help but remember the eggs we had in Kalovar, big brown eggs that sputtered in the cast-iron pan as they fried and the yolk so yellow-orange and delicious. But these pale eggs I could not touch. Nor could the others.

We sat around the table, four gloomy people sipping tea in a dark crowded apartment. I wanted to open the curtains to let the daylight in but Mama was afraid. "People would look in on us as they walked by."

"Remember how. . . ." Already that dangerous word appeared. We remembered how the morning sun streamed through the paned windows when we woke up in the early hours, how the little birds were forever twittering in the grapevines, the smell of baking bread from the kitchen, the familiar bowl of yogurt, perhaps a basket of plums or cherries, and always rolls and tea. Mirjana, the artist of the family, insisted on arranging a bouquet of flowers though Mama sometimes scolded her, "Is that all you have to do?" Now we missed the flowers. We missed the rolls and the jam and everything else. I even felt pangs of affection for those silly chickens who tried to hide their eggs from us by laying them in the bushes or wherever they thought we wouldn't find them. If only I had one of their golden eggs now, how grateful I would be!

"I wish they had let us keep the food we brought with us," Marko said mournfully.

"I cannot understand what's happened to Nevenka," Mama mused. "She used to be such a good cook. Has she forgotten?"

"I don't understand it either," Mirjana said. "Maybe we didn't look hard enough. Wait!"

She went to the kitchen and we heard the refrigerator door open, then some drawers in the cupboard. "Wait, wait!" Mirjana cried and then brought over to the table a bag of rolls, such as we always had at home, a large piece of cheese, a plate of thinly sliced meat, a jar of plum jam and a coffee cake. Beautiful food!

"We must be blind," Mirjana said. "Aunt Nevenka left all this here for us but it was wrapped so carefully we didn't even notice it. And we didn't open all the cupboards or all the drawers. She even made stuffed cabbage for us!"

Now we had breakfast. Good Croatian food, not quite the same as it was at home, but close enough so that we felt some of Croatia was still with us.

"How could we have missed it before," Mirjana said, "when it was there right in front of our eyes?"

"Because," Mama began, and I knew we would be treated to proverbs and even a lecture such as Papa might have given at such a time, "we were looking only at our own misery. If you look for misery, you get misery. If you are hopeful, good things come to you."

"Maybe," Mirjana said as she buttered a piece of crumb cake, but suddenly tears filled her eyes. "Even so, I want to go back to Kalovar. I think we should all go back there."

"And where would we go?" Mama asked so sadly that I suspected the same thought had occurred to her. "The Inn is sold. The house belongs to someone else, the orchard, the fields, the goats . . . all gone now."

In a minute I would be crying too along with them. But Marko saved us as he cried, *"Zivalee!"* Unable to stand our complaints, he was monkeying around with the black and white television set that Aunt Nevenka let us use, now that she had a colored TV, and soon he was tuned in to a hockey game. Now nothing in all the world would drag him back to Kalovar.

I jumped up from the table. "Marko is right! He is looking for what he wants here. Why we haven't even been outside yet! We haven't seen Canada, only this little place. It's beautiful by the Bay. Come on, let's all go outside and see what it's like."

"You're right, Danica, good for you! You have more sense than we do," Mama admitted. "No more talk of Kalovar. It's over. And you, Mirjana, not one more tear. You hear me? No more weeping."

Mama stood up, her shoulders straight. Once more this was the Mama who had to be strong because she was both father and mother now. Mirjana blew her nose in one last long, decisive blast and dabbed at her eyes, but said nothing.

Mama promised she would take a walk later, but soon Aunt Nevenka and Uncle Ivo would be coming to help straighten out the myriad of things that had to be done, so I went out by myself.

The sky was pale, nearly colorless, and the street empty excepting for two old ladies with shopping bags, one of whom said "Good morning" to me as she passed. "That's friendly!" I thought.

Birds chirped in the naked branches of the trees. I stopped to wonder at a seagull who cried his melancholy note as he swooped down and then up again to disappear among the tall towers. I walked down to the bottom of the hill, had my first daylight look at English Bay and then I knew I would stay here forever. Quiet water glistened in the morning light, and rippling in small rounded waves caught jewels of sunlight even though I could not find the sun in the sky. In the distance where the Bay widened to become the ocean, I counted at least four large ships, and as there were too many sailboats to count, I stood there admiring them as they slanted in the breeze. The water became deeply blue farther out and even bluer were the islands and hills, folding gracefully one behind the other until the one farthest away was as pale as the sky.

"Wait till Mama sees this!"

After our cramped rooms, this expanse of space would be sheer heaven.

The small waves lapped up on a sandy beach, above which was a long promenade that bordered green grass and clumps of trees, a long pleasant park, bounded by an avenue on which could be seen the high-rise buildings, all of them higher than I had expected, gleaming white in the gray morning light. At the base of each were carpets of lawn and carefully planted gardens. I remembered what my teacher called this view when he saw it on a postcard. "The Riviera of the North!"

The sun came out from behind a cloud, shining with triumph as it lit up the edges of the trees, and made the water so suddenly bright it hurt my eyes to look at it. Two young men jogged along the seawall. An older woman and one not much older than Mirjana, both of them dressed smartly in pants and jacket, were taking their dogs out for a walk. An old man walked by himself, then stopped and stretched out his arm while birds flew down to peck at the seeds he held in his hand.

"Beautiful! So beautiful!"

It was the only word I could think of to explain how I felt about it. Kalovar is beautiful too, a small voice said inside of me, as though I were unfaithful. Yes, I argued with that voice, but this is beautiful in a different way. And this is my new home.

Vancouver, how I love the sound of the word! How I love this place! Vancouver!

We were here at last and I was glad.

When I got home I found Uncle Ivo sitting on a chair, one leg crossed over the other, and I wondered if the poor chair would survive under his weight. He was smoking a long, black cigar and from time to time took the slimy thing from his mouth, regarded the end of it approvingly, then put it back in his mouth. Aunt Nevenka was knitting something and Mirjana sat at the table, writing down notes and apparently figuring a budget as Uncle Ivo talked. But Mama, who always sat proud and erect, nearly slumped in her chair and covered her eyes with her hands as if she were trying to think. Immediately I could see she was discouraged.

"Dinars, dollars, dollars, dinars . . . it's all so confusing," she said. "I know one thing, whether you call it dollars or whatever, I'll never be able to manage the rent. Ivo, whatever made you think I had so much money? What kind of robbers make us pay so much for this . . . this basement?"

"Nadja, rents everywhere are high. This is as low as you will get and you are lucky to find a place at all. Trust me, sister, trust me. Your job will take care of the rent and food while you get acquainted here. It's different here, not like Croatia, not like a small country village. First you will learn English at free classes. You will find out how it is to live in this city. And then we will find a place for the restaurant and the money will come in. You will laugh at how afraid you are today. Your children will grow up Canadian."

A new worry for Mama. "But they are Croatian; I wouldn't want them to forget."

"Not a chance," Uncle Ivo said. "We have ten thousand Croatians here, societies, clubs, the church. Don't worry, they don't have to forget."

He talked glibly, as though he hadn't a worry in the world and neither should we. Then he looked at his watch. "Come, Nadja, we have to go to the Immigration Office and take care of many matters."

Mama left reluctantly, full of advice: we mustn't let strangers in, mustn't get lost, mustn't . . . a hundred "mustn'ts." After they left, Mirjana said to me, "Danica, I don't care what Uncle Ivo says. Once we get that restaurant opened and Mama can take care of herself, I'm going back to Kalovar, I'm going to marry Mirko."

"Well, send me a postcard," I retorted unsympathetically.

One thing was certain. *I* wasn't going back. It would not be easy in Vancouver, but this is where I would stay.

CHAPTER 13

At four o'clock one afternoon, I sat at home alone waiting for the others to show up. Sitting at the table, I bit the tip of my pen wondering what I could write to Tanja. We had been in Vancouver two weeks, and though I'd promised to write, I had not yet sent a letter. I read what I'd written:

Dear Tanja:

It is the most beautiful place in the world, lovelier than I dreamed it would be, better than the postcards . . .

What my pen wanted to say was this:

Dear Tanja:

Yes, it's beautiful, but I want to go back to Kalovar. I wish I'd never left it. It's not easy being here.

Nothing in the world would get me to write that.

It was true that Vancouver was a beautiful place. To see the sun shining on the Bay and the gulls wheeling overhead made my heart lift until I felt as if I too could fly. But for a week now it was glum, sunless, and the air was thick. Everything was light gray or dark gray and as void of color as the images on our television. We could not see the blue mountains that guarded the northern boundaries of Vancouver, and even the water of the Bay was a listless gray.

At that point in my musing, Mama came in and put a small brown bag of groceries on the table. When I saw how she looked, I forgot to feel sorry for myself. "Five dollars," she said. "Five dollars for that little bag of food!" She collapsed on a chair, limp and weary.

"Mamo, you work too hard, You never used to be this tired back home and you worked all the time there."

"Don't worry about it, Danica. I'll get used to it. Someday. How was school today?"

I did not answer. "Let me take off your shoes, Mamo. Want me to rub your ankles? It will make them feel better."

"If you want . . ." and as I massaged her aching feet and propped them up on a chair for her, she patted my head, "Danica, you have magic fingers. My poor feet feel better already. But I'll just sit for a while."

I put away the groceries, then put hot water on for a soothing cup of tea for her. "Mamo, tell me, are the people you work for mean to you? Do they say anything?"

"Sure, they say lots of things but they say them in English, so I don't understand. Men don't like to see a woman chef. They think I should only be washing dishes, so they are resentful. The boss, he is pleased. . . . Don't worry, Danica."

Mama had never complained this much. Even when her job discouraged her, she admitted nothing. Besides, what could we do about it? Mama was used to being her own boss; other jobs were not easy to find; and although she went to English class every afternoon after work, still she could not learn the language all at once.

"Someday, it will be better," she sighed and I wondered if she really believed it.

Just then Mirjana came in, followed a few minutes later by Marko, who banged his way in noisily. His face was rosy and shiny after an afternoon of soccer with his friends. Of all of us, he was happiest in our new country. Mirjana had plunged herself into language studies. "We'll never get anywhere if we don't learn the language."

"We must speak to each other in English," she had declared, "so we will get used to it." We tried, finding it easier to laugh at ourselves than to speak in front of others. But when we were very tired, it was good to talk in our native language.

"Listen to me, Alex has invited me to his house for dinner tomorrow," Marko cried. "Can I go, eh, can I go?"

Even though he spoke Croatian, he was learning to include the "eh" which I sometimes heard in Canadian speech.

"Good, you are making new friends. Yes, you can go," Mama said, "but remember your good manners."

He whooped with happiness and turned on the television. Mirjana kissed Mama on the forehead and said, "You sit there now and take it easy. I'm going to make dinner tonight, and guess who's going to help."

At home I would have stuck out my tongue at her, but now it felt so comforting for all of us to be together after the long afternoon and to speak Croatian instead of English that I surprised Mirjana by embracing her and kissing her. Suddenly relieved, I'm not sure why, I hugged Mama and then went to embrace Marko.

"Oh no, you don't!" he cried and I chased him through the house. When I caught him I tickled him and we both fell to the floor giggling.

"That's more like it," Mama said. "It's almost like home after all."

The next afternoon I was determined to finish the letter to Tanja. All I could think of were complaints:

It's not quite what we expected. For example, we are lonely. Mama gets up early each day and sees that we have breakfast, as we did at home. But then she goes off to work; Mirjana straightens the apartment and then goes off to school, which is far away for her; Marko goes to his school and I go to mine. Three different schools. For a whole day we are separated. In Kalovar there was always someone home and if one of us was gone, we never worried because we knew where everyone was. But this is a big city, and poor Mama worries the most; where is Marko in all this vastness, where is Mirjana, where is Danica?

Maybe we will get used to it. It takes time.

Only I was too proud to write that to Tanja. I put away the letter for another day, then took it out again as I realized she would want to know about the schools here. What should I tell her?

On the first two days we were here, Aunt Nevenka drove us around the city so we could get acquainted and see the sights, but on the third day we had to begin school. First Marija took Marko to the grammar school and saw that he was settled; then we walked on farther to the King George Secondary School, which was about three times as large as the school in Kalovar. Marija took me to the office, introduced me to the principal and helped me answer his questions but then she had to leave to take Mirjana to her classes in another part of the city. "Will you be able to find your way home?" Marija asked me to my embarrassment, as if I were a baby, and then she left.

The principal, a very kind man, spoke so slowly that I could almost understand what he said. The halls were filled with students going to one class or another—it is so different from Kalovar where we have only ONE class for everyone—and I expected to join them, but he took me to a room and said, "This is where you will be. It is a class for people who do not speak English, or well—who need a little practice." Perhaps I turned red, for he added tactfully, "As soon as you are ready, you may go to regular classes."

In a few days, I was thinking, surely I'll be one of the regular students.

The teacher was such a young man I was surprised. Our teacher in Kalovar was much older, a tall bony man with a beard. Mr. Robson, my new teacher, introduced me to the ten students in the class, some of them Pakistani, a few from Africa, one from Chile, three Chinese boys—all of them foreigners like me. How kind everyone was, how encouraging! Mr. Robson made it easy for us to understand and to speak and encouraged us all to listen to radio or television. He was so tactful that I thought to myself, I'm not so bad after all. In a few days I shall be with real Canadians.

A loud bell rang, stinging the air, and George, a Chinese boy, explained it was lunchtime, so copying the others I followed everyone to the cafeteria, which was very crowded. I stood in line, bought soup, being very proud that I could manage without any difficulty, and then I sat at a long table with nine students who were genuine Canadians. They talked very fast and laughed a great deal, horsing around as we sometimes did back home. Then a girl turned to me.

"Hello, you're new, aren't you? I'm Sheila Blandford."

Perhaps she did not think I was foreign, for she seemed surprised when I spoke in what I suppose must be an accent. "I'm Danica Pavelic."

"Who?" she frowned.

"Danica Pavelic. From Croatia. Yugoslavia."

"That's great. I hope you will like it here."

She said some more but I didn't understand, for she spoke so fast. Apparently she was introducing me to the others at the table and I nodded to each one; a boy whistled, I didn't know why, and a girl said "Shut up" to still another boy.

"Do you speak English at all?" someone asked. But I had to ask the boy, "Please, would you repeat?" and some other people talked with me, but it was no use. I could not understand. I sat there wishing that my clothes were like theirs and that I could speak fast like them and that I were not such a foreigner. At last several of them got up to leave and the others followed. "See ya," some of them said, a farewell I'd never learned, and I was left sitting alone. Alone and left out.

Then George, the Chinese boy, slipped in on the bench beside me.

"Hello," he said.

"Hello, George."

Now I have the feeling that he had seen what was going on and that he understood how discouraged I was. But he tapped on his wristwatch. "Time to go back," he said.

On the stairs he said, "Every day it will get more easy for you."

He was very kind, and when we went back to class, it was like going back to a little home in this place that was so far from home.

It would never do to put all this in a letter, so instead I wrote:

Everyone here wears very stylish clothes, shirts, jeans, swingy skirts. The stores are filled with so many marvelous things to wear, already made, that I can't make up my mind which dresses and skirts to choose. It's not a real problem actually, because they cost a great deal of money and I don't have any of that!

You would like it very much, Tanja. Like me, you would never get your fill of lovely things.

How are the goats, Tanja? I know you will take good care of them. Tell me, how is dear Snowball? When you milk her, whisper in her ear that I love her and that I miss her . . .

But I could not finish the letter because when I thought of Snowball and of Tanja, the lonesomeness welled up in me, an ache like no ache I have ever had, an ache so deep I couldn't even cry about it. If only I could wake up in my own bed back home and know all this was only a dream, I would never leave Croatia again.

But I was not back in my wooden bed under the casement windows, and this was not a dream. Vancouver was real and I was here. I put the letter away for another time and began to prepare dinner.

The next day I added more to the letter. Perhaps I lingered in writing it because in a way it was like being with Tanja.

One way or another, we are actually learning English. Mirjana is determined to speak perfectly and when she puts her mind to something, everyone else must watch out! She may look soft and weepy but she is relentless. Even now she is planning to take business courses as soon as her English is advanced enough.

Marko picks it up easily as if it were a native tongue. Sometimes he does too well, and repeats words he learned on the playground, bad words. Mama is not quite sure that she understands, but Mirjana knows and says she will wash his mouth out with soap if he uses them again.

Sometimes Mama goes to very intense English classes at a place near where she works, but several nights a week she goes to a community house where the feeling is easier. It is not easy for her and we have to be careful not to laugh at her when she mixes up her words, because she sometimes makes funny mistakes. When I think of it, I begin to worry and wonder if perhaps I do not make funny mistakes as well.

There was something more that I wanted to say, yet I couldn't think what it might be, so the letter remained unfinished.

Everything was beginning to go a little better. I was beginning to love our class, where we sometimes put on little plays or skits and had little games and spelling bees that helped us learn more quickly. Sometimes we took our lunch to school and went to Stanley Park, only a few blocks away, where we had picnics. However, I was still far from "being a Canadian."

When school was over, I didn't know what to do. Nobody would be at home and rather than sit there in that dark living room, I walked through the park and up and down the streets, memorizing their names, Denman, Broughton, Nicola, Burnaby, Bute. . . . I shivered in my detested brown coat and wondered if spring would ever come.

The cherry trees were flowering, and sometimes I came upon one of them, a mist of pink blossoms silhouetted against the cold blue of the distant mountains. Then I would think that nothing could be more lovely.

Not all the West End was made up of overpowering thirty-story buildings of cold concrete. Here and there among the skyscrapers were tucked small wooden houses with steep roofs, tiny irregular windows and old-fashioned porches. Some of these were painted proudly in peculiar colors, acid greens, dingy rusts and occasionally an unexpected shade of lavender. Others were unpainted, shabby and unloved, like sad old people who lingered around amazed at the way the world was changing. Yet some of these humble cottages were named as though they were mansions, *The Queen Elizabeth, Stuart Lodge* and *Herrington Hall.* An abandoned house, once painted pink, and now a residence for pigeons that went in and out of the gabled windows, bore the impressive title *Kensington Manor.*

Uncle Ivo said that one day many of these small houses would be torn down to make way for more high apartment houses. Even some of the older wooden mansions would give way to the rich barons who would have them leveled "in one hour flat," Uncle Ivo boasted, "thanks to modern machinery." It was not easy to be small and poor; these houses were country relatives, like us.

Once in a while when Mirjana walked with me we could choose our favorite buildings and say the splendid names out loud. Elizabeth Court, Winthrop Manor, The Barcelona, The St. Pierre, Englesea Lodge. Every place had its name, as if the words "château, villa, lodge, court and manor" could give us the illusion of being in England, France or Spain.

We never tired of watching the buildings, the Bay, the

sailboats, and above all the people. In Kalovar everyone was more or less alike, but here was a variety of people that left us open-mouthed. Walking down David Street, we saw a family of East Indians with the women wearing saris, three Chinese women and their babies, college students with pictures painted or embroidered on their jeans, a pair of well-groomed and tastefully attired ladies with white hair (whom we called Mrs. British Columbia!) . . . there was no end to it. And then there were the snatches of language we caught as we walked—French, Roumanian, Czech, Greek, German, English and many we could not identify. I could never be bored in such a place, and even Mirjana was caught up in the excitement of this cosmopolitan parade.

Yet as Mirjana grew more and more busy with school and seeing Marija, I walked by myself. In those slow afternoon hours, I looked in shop windows or lingered in the park to watch the children at the playground or the ducks on the pond. One afternoon as I drifted toward home, something stopped me in my tracks. There on a bench, calmly smoking and looking out over the Bay was a girl I knew, someone dear, someone unexpected. I even heard snatches of popular music from a transistor radio that she held.

Tanja, it was Tanja! Hard to believe, but it had to be Tanja. I was so certain that I almost cried out her name. But still what was she doing here in a long cotton dress, a green jacket and long scarf, sitting on that bench and smoking! Tanja smoking?

I walked closer. The girl on the bench turned around and then it was clear that, of course, it wasn't Tanja at all. That girl, whoever she was, had the same high forehead and a certain curve of cheek that made her resemble my friend, yet nobody could have been more unlike Tanja.

Disappointed, I dragged myself home, lonelier than ever. Counting my favorite houses, watching people rushing home with bags of groceries under their arms, and even smiling at the Chinese woman who owned the corner grocery and always grinned at me, was all well and good, but not enough. I wanted a friend. A real friend. A friend like Tanja.

Then I knew how to finish the letter, and I finished it.

I miss you very much, Tanja. There is no friend here like you. "Don't forget" you embroidered on the kerchief you gave me. Did you think I could ever forget you! Could I ever forget Kalovar! Never, I assure you. I would like nothing more than to see you again. I send you my love,

Danica.

CHAPTER 14

"You're becoming Canadian all right and I'm not sure I like it. You, Danica, are becoming GREEDY! You were never like this in Kalovar."

"Mamo, it's different here. Can't you understand? There it didn't matter. Here you have to look nice, have good clothes. See how I'm growing out of this sweater. Just take a look."

I pushed my arms forward so that the sweater seemed smaller than it really was, and I held my dress in back so that its very tightness would shock Mama into insisting I wear something "more decent and modest." But she wasn't fooled.

"I want a bike, Mamo. All the other kids have them. And if Danica has new clothes, then I should have a new bike," Marko argued.

"Shame on both of you. Can't you see Mama's tired? She works all day. Besides, there isn't any money, so keep quiet, will you? We are lucky if we can pay rent." Mirjana was right to scold us. We were being selfish.

What happened was that on my lonely afternoons I looked in the windows of the dress shops along Davie Street and Denman Street, and I never got over believing how wonderful it was that one could go inside, try on a dress and walk out wearing it. One only had to pay for it. At home the dressmaker from the next village made your clothes and told you what to wear, with set ideas about what was proper for you, and you had nothing to say about it. It was hopeless. Here I longed for hundreds of things but would have settled for a certain blue dress with tiny sprigs of flowers printed all over it.

"Mamo, if you would just look in the window of Trudi's Shop, you'd see this sweet blue dress. You'd be proud to see me in it."

Mama wavered. "How much is it, this dress?"

"Twenty-five dollars, that's all."

"Twenty-five dollars!" Mama's English lapsed back into Croatian where she translated dollars into dinars and then back again with a shocked expression on her face. "Twenty-five dollar! Too much. Why, when I was girl, I would not ask twenty-five cents."

"Okay, okay, OKAY," I said in defeat, glowering as I bit my thumb. I had to have new clothes. Then I would have friends. Nobody wanted to be seen with a girl whose clothes looked like potato sacks.

Two days later Mama came home from work, sat down to rub her tired feet, but her face was full of smiles. She had something to tell me, she said.

"You're going to buy me a dress?" Foolish Danica!

"Not quite. But you will have a new dress! There is a class in sewing and Nevenka says I can have her old sewing machine because she has a new one. Is old-fashioned, she says, but works good. I make you a dress."

"That's nice," I said, trying to sound more enthusiastic, and still wishing she would buy the dress. Mama could weave well and embroider better than anyone in the village but she had never made modern clothes before, only costumes. "Will you make the dress just like the one in Trudi's Shop?"

"Sure, Danica, anything you want."

"Mamo, you are so wonderful!" I hugged her. Then I told her exactly how the dress should be made, how the waist must fit, how the skirt must swirl out, how the collar should fit, what kind of buttons it must have. "Yes, yes," she agreed. We even went to look at the dress in Trudi's Shop, and Mama promised she would copy it exactly.

Darling Mama! Though she was usually tired after work, she went to sewing class after English class, three times a week. It seemed as though I would become an old lady before the dress was ever finished, and Mirjana warned me not to ask Mama all the time when it would be done.

At last she came home one night with a Hudson Bay shopping bag which she placed reverently in my arms. She looked so proud, I threw my arms around her neck and kissed her.

"Mamo. Thank you, thank you."

"You're welcome. Enough kissing. Open up the bag. You'll see, it's just what you asked."

But instead of a dress with dainty flowers printed on it, Mama chose a brilliant blue material with enormous daisies five inches across. She did not skimp on the cloth; it was not cheap, only badly designed. As for the dress, it was enormous, the waist was at least five inches too large and the full skirt I wanted hung straight. Should I laugh or should I cry?

"Mamo, how could you?"

"Danica, you don't like it? This is what you wanted. The teacher says to make it longer here, shorter there; she knows what's right. Look how nice I made the seams. Danica, what's the matter?"

I ran to my room, slammed the door, and threw myself sobbing on the bed. Why did everything have to work out wrong? How could Mama have so little feeling for clothes when I had such a flair for fashion!

It wasn't fair. I hated being an immigrant, a foreigner from a far-off country that no one had heard of. Never did I feel less Canadian than at that moment. I could hear Mama asking Mirjana in puzzled tones, "What is the matter? What's wrong? It's just what she wanted."

"It's not," I cried, going back to the living room. Of course Aunt Nevenka had to choose precisely this minute to knock on the door and walk in. Between Mama's bewildered explanations and my red eyes, she sized up the situation.

"What a lovely dress!" she said to soothe Mama. "Beautiful. Come, Danica, try it on. How do you know what it's like until you put it on? Your Mama's worked so hard."

Without grace or thanks, I snatched the dress, knowing it was rude and unkind, yet I could not help it. I put on the detested dress, which hung down on both sides as though it were made for a woman forty years old. My sullen expression made it appear even uglier.

"Well, it is a little big," Mama admitted. "We could pull it in with a belt."

More tears ran down my cheeks. But Aunt Nevenka came to my rescue. "You know, Nadja," she advised my mother in soft-spoken tones, "you should stay with your cooking. There's not a better cook in the world. Or you could weave; ach, what a beautiful weaver you are. But leave dressmaking to someone else."

I was hoping that Aunt Nevenka would say, "Poor child, here's the money. Go buy yourself a dress." Instead she came into the bedroom as I was taking off the hated object. "Let me tell your Uncle Ivo and see if he has some ideas about how you can make a few dollars. He understands what it's like to be a young person and want new clothes. You mustn't be discouraged, Danica. When you're young, you want everything you see. Someday you will have it. In the meanwhile, Uncle Ivo will think of something."

How easy it was for her to talk like that! She had everything she wanted, but I could not wait until I was forty years old. I wanted to have the best of everything right now, yet I felt as if I had nothing.

What a miserable Danica I was becoming!

CHAPTER 15

Yet I had enough confidence in Uncle Ivo to stay home the next two days in case he called to tell me how I could make a hundred dollars in a hurry. By the third day, I figured he'd forgotten all about me.

Mirjana and I were home alone, that night while Mama was attending a class at the Neighborhood House and Marko was invited out to dinner at still another friend's house. Lucky Marko. Lucky Mirjana! She sat at the table with piles of colored crepe paper, wires and glue, humming as she made paper flowers. They were gaudy but actually very pretty, and she worked fast; as the old phrase goes, she had "a devil in her fingers."

The television was on, but I did not see it, did not hear it. I slumped in the one easy chair.

"Come on, Danica, why don't you make some flowers too?" she asked.

"You're the artist, not me," I answered glumly.

"Don't be silly. This isn't so hard. I don't know what you're so unhappy about, Danica. You were the one who wanted to come to Vancouver. But you're changing."

"And not for the better," she might have added. I used to be so happy and I never worried about money; there wasn't any to worry about in Kalovar. There I dreamed about big things, like becoming a doctor; here, I never thought of it.

Yet Mirjana, who had begged to stay home, was the most hopeful one of all of us. She was speaking English very well now and would soon begin her business courses. A group of girls who sang Croatian and Bulgarian folk songs had begged her to join their group. And other friends had asked her to take a course in making paper flowers and now here she was, happily turning them out.

"Maybe they're a little too gaudy, eh, Danica?" she asked, holding up a red poppy. "But they'll brighten this room, won't they? Next I'm going to do all the spring flowers we used to have back home, the lilies, the poppies, the daisies, the crocuses. Then we won't miss them so much. Maybe I'll be able to sell some too."

No wonder everyone spoke well of Mirjana. "Such a sweet girl," Aunt Nevenka had said, "A jewel of a girl. She never complains, always sees the bright side."

Mama told me that when Aunt Nevenka said that, my lower lip stuck out in a way that was not at all pretty and showed I was jealous. Well, I didn't care, I said. Let Mirjana make her flowers and sing her songs, tra-la-la; let her wear her hair up on top of her head like some bumpkin that just came in from the country; let her wear her thick stockings and that lumpy skirt that makes her look shorter and dumpier than ever. Let her write to her beloved Mirko three times a week for all I cared.

She might go back but not me. I wanted so much to be Canadian in every way, and yet it was so difficult. I felt as though I were nowhere, not back in Croatia and yet not quite here either, but hovering somewhere between the two. "I know it's not easy to be thirteen," Mirjana remarked sympathetically as though I were suffering from a dreadful disease. "If only you would get out a little more, try to make friends. . . ." She had so much advice I wanted to throw something at her.

Yet I gave in the night she invited me to a rehearsal of Pjevaj, the song group she had joined. "Why don't you come, Danica? They said you're welcome to sing with us, and besides you could help translate some of the Croatian songs."

"If they aren't Croatian, why do they bother to sing those songs?"

"Because the songs are beautiful. They really are. Don't you think it's remarkable that Canadian girls should love our music? Many of them dance too."

She had said the magic word that made me agree to go. They were Canadians.

"It's fun being there, like practicing for the Folk Festivals back home."

On Wednesday night we took a bus, transferred to another bus and traveled to a distant part of Vancouver where there are no high buildings at all but many small bungalow houses like the ones that were left standing in the West End. There was something comforting about these places with their porches, small lawns and gardens and the tall trees that grew along the street. Children played in the street, which made it seem comfortable and somehow familiar.

We walked up to the second floor of one of the houses. "Mirjana! Hello! Come in. How are you?"

A girl with a wide Slavic face and a head of thick auburn hair cried from the top of the stairs. "You've brought your sister! That's wonderful!"

As my sister had promised, the room was typically that of a student. Two mattresses on the floor were covered with handwoven blankets that were very different from those we had in Croatia; later I learned these came from Mexico. The room was crammed with pillows, baskets, weavings I recognized as coming from Zagreb, a bouzouki from Greece, a guitar, even a Macedonian bagpipe. More wonderful than any of that was a modern stereo with a long row of records on the floor beside it. There must have been a hundred records! With a set like that, I'd be able to learn all the latest songs. But as I was introduced I heard the record they played, some old recording made by a Bulgarian shepherd.

"Isn't it great?" one of the girls asked.

The group could not have been kinder. They said they were glad I came, please would I sing with them, and best of all they pronounced my name correctly. Dá-ni-tsa and not Day-ni-ka which was how the few Canadians I had met pronounced it.

Yet kind as they were, I didn't come to Canada to sing Croatian songs. Besides, they were all older than I, some of them at least twenty. So I listened.

To tell the truth, they were better than I expected. They sang easily and sometimes moved around as they sang, their voices sweet and strong and exactly right. Balkan songs are sung with a voice that is very different from that used in American and other Western countries.

They sang a few songs they knew well and then tried a new one. The one they chose was not even easy for the singers back home, and though they did well for Canadians, in one place they faltered. Without even thinking, I began to sing along with Mirjana to help them get over the difficult spots.

"Danica, you're great. You'll have to join the group," one of them said.

"We would be very pleased if you would," the Japanese girl said.

"Why don't you?" Mirjana asked on the way home. "Then you won't be so lonely."

In spite of my decision not to cling to things Croatian, I

wanted to say yes, but the Pavelic family is stubborn and I would not admit I'd enjoyed singing the old songs again.

"They're your friends, not mine," I told Mirjana.

"It doesn't matter."

"I'll find my own friends, thank you," I said coldly.

"Danica, what's happening to you? You must be homesick and unhappy. Sometimes I am too, but when I sing, all the unhappiness goes out of me and I feel light once more."

"Good for you, and your old songs. But I'm interested in *Canadian* songs," I said, looking out of the window, and then spitting out the final insult. "Besides, you're all so old!"

"Sourball!" Mirjana said. "Stay by yourself then. See if I care."

What's wrong with me, I wondered miserably as we walked the few blocks home after the bus stopped, apart and silent. I liked the girls; I loved their strange little apartment so full of things; and it was good to sing the songs again. I had wanted to join the group all along, but guessed now it was too late to change my mind and I was too stubborn to apologize to Mirjana and tell her she was right.

As we walked downstairs toward our suite, we sniffed a familiar odor. Cigar smoke. "Uncle Ivo?"

Sure enough, there he was sitting at the table with Aunt Nevenka and Mama, all of them drinking hot tea and nibbling Aunt Nevenka's incomparable coffee buns. Uncle Ivo beamed at both of us.

"Look at those beautiful girls! Come sit down with us. Danica, I came to talk with you. I've got a proposition for you."

What was "a proposition"? I didn't know, but I pulled up a chair and waited to hear what he had to say.

CHAPTER 16

Dear Uncle Ivo and his "gonnections!" He sucked his cigar, looked at it with satisfaction, put it back in his mouth and let it move up and down as he talked. "A big shot," as Marko said, but I didn't care.

"You want to make a little money, eh? Hard to find jobs now."

"I know."

"Hard for young girls to find jobs, especially young girls who've just come over."

I nodded. How long would it be before he got to the point?

"It's hard, but your Uncle Ivo found a little job for you. How would you like to walk a dog?"

"Walk a dog, Uncle Ivo?" I must have looked perplexed, never having heard of such a thing. He laughed.

"Sure, in Kalovar you never heard that kind of talk. Dogs could walk by themselves. But here when people live in suites sometimes they are too busy to take their dogs outside for exercise or . . . other purposes. I don't have to explain to you. Dogs are the same here as in Kalovar in that respect. Anyway, now and then someone hires a person to take the dog out for a walk every day and save them the trouble."

"That's the job? Someone would pay me money to take a dog out for a walk? But I love dogs. I'd do that for nothing."

"No, no, no, no, NO!" Uncle Ivo shook his head and his jowls quivered. "When you work, you get paid. Don't forget that. But you must also give service, be responsible, keep the dog on the leash and show up every day. You understand?"

"Oh yes, Uncle Ivo."

"All right then. I know a doctor, a nice man, highly respected, and he said he would like to have someone walk his dog each day. I'll write down the name and address for you, and this is the apartment number. Have you gone up in any of the high rises?"

I shook my head no.

"What you do, Danica, is you ring the bell, listen at the telephone there; a voice will ask Yes, who is it? and you will tell him your name and that you're Ivo Markota's niece. Then he will push a buzzer and you can open the door and go in. Go up on the elevator; he will interview you and maybe give you the job."

"How much is he going to pay?" Marko asked. Mama looked embarrassed.

"I don't know, something, but you won't get rich right away. Remember, Danica, it's a privilege for a young girl to have any kind of job. Try it for a while, and if it goes well, your Uncle Ivo has a great idea for you . . ."

He winked to show that he knew all the angles and all the "gonnections" and I was lucky to have someone like Uncle Ivo.

"If you like that kind of work, you can put an ad in the local newspaper that everyone reads here in the West End and get yourself more jobs."

"Uncle Ivo, you are wonderful!" I cried, hugging him

and trying to avoid his smelly cigar at the same time. "You're so good to me."

"Well, it's a pleasure to do something for a pretty niece. And it's good to have the fine Pavelic family here. I like ambitious people."

"At least it's good to see you smiling again, Danica," Mama said. "And now, please put up another kettle of water for more tea, will you?"

As I stood in the kitchen, watching the kettle heat the water, I wondered what I should buy first, once I was paid, a pair of jeans, high-heel sandals or a new dress. Then I thought of more things I wanted and before I knew it the water in the kettle had all boiled away. I began again, and this time I paid attention to what I was doing.

The one thing about Canada that set both Mirjana and myself into giggling fits was the sight of people walking with big dogs or tiny little pooches straining at the end of a leash. Some wore jeweled collars; others wore hand-knit sweaters or plaid blankets. Such dogs, of course, could never drive sheep or guard property such as the big, burly dogs we had at home. Nor could Mirjana and I believe that section of the supermarket where row after row of foods, biscuits, canned meats and even special candy were displayed for dog and cat owners to buy for their pets, and even more unbelievable was the display of baskets to be used as dog beds, toys, rubber bones, felt mice filled with catnip, shampoos, powders and soaps.

But if someone was foolish enough to want to pay me to take a dog for a walk, I was not about to argue or criticize.

Dr. Weiss lived in one of the most elegant of all the high-rise towers, not far from Stanley Park. Pink and lavender azaleas bloomed profusely in the gardens that edged the well-kept lawns at the base of Wellington Towers. Following Uncle Ivo's directions, I pressed the lever at 2001, which meant Dr. Weiss lived on the twentieth floor. Nervously I held the telephone receiver to my ear.

"Yes, what can I do for you?" The voice, strongly accented, sounded as though the speaker were Austrian.

"I am Danica Pavelic. My uncle, Ivo Markota, sent me."

"Ah, yes! Very goot. Come up then."

Like the fairy tale "Open Sesame," the buzzer rang and I opened the heavy glass door. The lobby was carpeted in thick red rugs, accented with tubs of rich green foliage, and made even more magnificent by crystal chandeliers that hung from the ceiling. I walked over to the two bronze doors which I supposed were the elevators. And there I stopped.

What was I supposed to do then?

It must seem unbelievable that at thirteen I did not know about such things as elevators. We did not use them in Kalovar. In Zagreb and Vancouver department stores I learned about escalators, but elevators . . . how did one open the doors? Should I press one of the two buttons alongside the door? Possibly, but which one? What if it were the one that rang an alarm that caused bells to ring and I would then be arrested for creating a false alarm? Then I had the happy solution that there must be stairs, not that I looked forward to walking up twenty flights but that was better than losing a job.

I looked around but could not find the stairs. And now what should I do? Dr. Weiss would be waiting for me and here I would stay forever! Tears began to sting my eyes, when a lady, one of those Mirjana and I call Mrs. British

Columbia, white hair pressed into even professional waves and curls, walked up to the elevator and pressed one of the buttons. A tiny poodle yapped at the end of his leash. Mrs. B.C., bless her, knew exactly what she was doing; no alarm bells rang, but the bronze doors parted with dignity and she stepped in the elevator. Taking my chances, I followed her.

"What floor?" she asked.

"Twenty, please," I whispered.

She pressed the button that said twenty and I thanked her, too profusely I'm afraid, for she nodded with a cold, dry smile that lasted less than a second. At the twelfth floor she sailed out, tugging the little dog behind her. Now I was alone in the elevator and I hoped it knew what it was doing, and indeed it did, for it stopped at twenty and the bronze doors opened for me as I walked into the corridor.

This one was covered with a thick carpet of red and gold diamond patterns. At the end of the corridor a large mirror in an elaborate gold frame reflected the girl from Kalovar who walked down the hall.

"That's me?" I was not used to such a grand mirror. "Not bad," for I was tall enough to be taken for sixteen or seventeen. The dark curly hair that came to my shoulders looked neat and presentable, but the white shirt and dark blue skirt were terrible. Really terrible. They made me look ten, barely eleven years old. Old-country clothes.

"But in a short while I'll buy something else," I assured myself as I rang the bell at the door marked 2001. Chimes played and a short round man with rimless glasses and a rosy face looked up at me.

"Hello, hello. Danica, is it? Come right in."

He led me into a small hall that opened on a living room, rich with Oriental rugs, paintings and furniture covered with plush brown velvet. If it weren't for the wide modern windows, the room might have been in a highly cultured European house. Glass-fronted cabinets displayed fragile china and figurines; bookcases lined some of the walls; and a grand piano, a Bechstein, filled a corner. The pale blue sky that sported pearly gray clouds was framed like a painting between the transparent curtains that hung from ceiling to floor, behind mauve velvet drapes.

"Have a seat, Danica," Dr. Weiss indicated a chair at his walnut desk. His white hair that curved over his collar made him look very nice and grandfatherly. And his gray eyes sparkled as if he were amused, but yet there was a hint of sadness in him. I wonder if he had been affected by the war. My father once said that anyone involved in that awful time would forever carry around a remnant of sorrow.

"Have you been in Canada very long, Danica?"

"Five weeks."

"And you go to school, h'm?"

"King George Secondary. I'm in the English course now, but in the fall I'll be in the regular classes . . . if I pass."

"Aha!" he said, as if now he understood everything. He sat with elbows on the desk, fingertips pressed together and regarded me through the shifting light of his glasses.

He was about to ask me something more when a small dog with curly gray hair, white whiskers and ears held high pranced into the room with careful steps. At first I thought he was a puppy but as he came over to me, it was clear he was a dignified aging poodle. He let me pet him, wagged his tail and did not leave.

"There, Budi approves of you!" Dr. Weiss said obviously pleased. "He doesn't take to everyone. Now where is . . . Anna!" he called.

"I'm coming, dear." Almost immediately a petite

woman, perhaps as old as Dr. Weiss though not so round, walked in from another room, taking many tiny steps on shoes with thin high heels. Her face was as rosy as her husband's and the white hair was charmingly pinned back into a chignon. She held out both hands to me as Dr. Weiss introduced her.

"I'm so happy that you are here," she said, "and I know that you and Budi will be great friends. Budi has been with us for many years now."

As she bent down to attach the leash to Budi's jeweled collar, I remembered that Aunt Nevenka once remarked that this dog was as dear to them as a child. The dog even *looked* like them. I wondered if "Budi" was a Hungarian or Roumanian name and I'm glad I did not ask, for later Uncle Ivo explained his name was the American "Buddy," but they did not pronounce it too well.

"Now then, Danica," Dr. Weiss explained. "We take Budi out a few times during the day, but what we want is for you to exercise him for at least half an hour a day. Don't run too fast, or walk too slow. Budi is not a young dog any more. You may take him to the park, and if he wants to stop and sniff a bush or take care of his private needs, that is his privilege. You understand?"

"Yes, Dr. Weiss."

"All right, then perhaps you should become acquainted with Budi and find out how you like each other. Then we can make arrangements."

Mrs. Weiss gave me the leash, smiled, walked me to the door as Budi trotted after us, and I was on my way.

Budi did not even seem as independent as our sheep dog, Stanko, back in Croatia, yet I liked him more than I expected. This city dog, this retired gentleman, bore a certain elegance, kept his tail high and, despite his apparent frailty, seemed glad to be alive.

What I had not expected was that he would bring me acquaintances. For the first time since I'd been in Vancouver, people passing by smiled at Budi and then nodded at me. It was hardly flattering to be thought of as someone who went with a dog rather than the other way around, but still I was grateful enough to smile back at anyone who said hello to me.

The half hour passed quickly. I glanced at the watch that Marija had given me, an old one she didn't use any more, and told Budi we had to go back. Once we were back in the Weisses' apartment he pranced around the living room on his hind legs in a spirited sort of way.

"Well, he hasn't done that for at least three years. You must have made him very happy."

And so the job was mine. Dr. Weiss told me how much he would pay me and asked if that were satisfactory. I could not believe my luck. Dr. Weiss beamed, Mrs. Weiss nodded and looked pleased, and I think my cheeks were burning.

I ran home tingling with joy.

CHAPTER 17

Seeing Dr. and Mrs. Weiss and walking Budi made up the happiest hour of the day. Yet when I sat down with a pencil to figure out how long it would take me to get the jeans I wanted, and a long skirt, and a jacket, I realized it would take five years of walking Budi to begin such a wardrobe.

Uncle Ivo's idea about placing an ad in the West End newspaper haunted me and I spent two evenings trying to word the ad correctly. Finally I had it. I walked to the office of the paper.

"Please, may I speak to the editor?"

"Sure. What can I do for you?"

"Would you print this ad?"

The editor read the paper I handed him and scratched his head.

Wanted to walk dogs. A girl. Reliable.

"Young lady, do you want to hire a girl to walk your dog?"

"No, of course not," I cried, shocked that he could interpret my ad in that way. "I want to walk other people's dogs. It's a job."

"Well, if you don't want dozens of girls beating down

your door, perhaps we'd better word this differently, and get your telephone number down too."

He rewrote the ad and then, although he was very young, he spoke to me seriously like a father or an uncle. "Make sure that whoever calls you really wants you to walk their dog. If someone wants to make a date with you or suggests anything else, hang up. Don't give your address to anyone. You have to be careful in a city like this."

Uncle Ivo had warned us all that the city could be a dangerous place and Aunt Nevenka had nodded solemnly in agreement. Outside I could see the sun shining on the Bay and a sailboat leaning in the breeze like a child's toy. What could possibly go wrong in a place as lovely as this?

"I'll be careful," I promised the editor, "and thanks for the help."

"You're welcome, and good luck!" he called out after me.

The advertisement brought two phone calls. The first came from a woman with a strong British accent and such a correct way of talking that I found myself saying, "Yes, ma'am," and "No, ma'am," even over the phone even though I don't usually talk that way. She could not pronounce my name; worse than anyone so far, she called it Dah-nye-kah!

This was Miss Agatha Hornby who lived in The Tudor, a long imposing house in the old English style, geometrical brown timbers placed against gray walls. Definitely not a high rise, this proud residence gave the impression of an upper-class English country house placed on a rolling lawn by the Bay. The yard was edged with precisely clipped hedges and the windows displayed window boxes of salmon-colored geraniums.

Miss Hornby, a dry, aging maiden lady whose gray hair was tied into a hard knot at the nape of her neck stood rigidly straight and did not smile as she examined me from head to toe. I squirmed under her glance; I should have polished my shoes before I left home, I should have pressed my skirt, I worried that my fingernails were not as clean as they should be. Miss Hornby told me she had for years been the headmistress of a private school for young ladies and had high expectations.

"And here is Lancelot!" she announced as a sad, comical beast ambled into the stiff living room where I stood with Miss Hornby. At first I thought this poor dog must have had an unfortunate choice of father and mother, for his long solid body and noble head were supported on feet that were ridiculously short and bowed for the bulk they supported. Miss Hornby read my mind.

"Young lady, Lancelot is a basset hound and he looks *exactly* the way a basset hound should look. Not only is he registered, but his family tree is one of the finest and oldest of the breed. I don't suppose you could trace your family back forty generations, could you?"

This last remark was meant to put me in my place, but it only made me angry. "I cannot speak for my personal family, but Croatia is one of the oldest European nations. Our first king was crowned in 925 and we had one of the first parliaments in Europe."

"Well, my dear, you do show spirit. I'm glad to see you have pride in your native country, Da-nye-kah."

"My name is pronounced *Da'nitza,*" I said softly, not wanting to correct her. After all, she could hardly be blamed for not speaking Croatian. "It means Morning Star."

"Yes, yes, that's interesting. Now then, let me tell you about Lancelot."

I stood erect while she lectured. "Lancelot must walk, walk, walk! You must not sit down, Da-nye-kah, nor stop to talk with anyone. Keep to the better side of the West End and yes, you may take him to the park. Lancelot must accomplish the 'purpose' of his walk. And of course you must speak to him in English; he hardly needs to learn a new language at this stage of his life."

"Yes, Miss Hornby."

The rates were the same as for Dr. Weiss. I was careful to follow her instructions. One day I happened to glance back at The Tudor and I found her standing at the window following us with binoculars! What did she expect me to DO with Lancelot?

One day I was two minutes late and Miss Hornby was highly displeased. "If you were a student at the school where I had the privilege of being headmistress, you would have received two misdemeanors for your tardiness. Time is money!"

I wondered if she would dock my pay, small as it was.

"I'm sorry," I said.

"Well, Lancelot seems to like you so much, we'll let it go this time."

"I like you too, old thing," I said to him as we walked down the promenade. It was true. I felt sorry for him too. At one time he must have been a vigorous creature, tracking down badgers or foxes or other woodland animals. Even now, when he saw a black squirrel in the park, he nearly pulled me after him in his effort to chase it. It always made me happy to see him become spirited, because his life at The Tudor must have been very dull.

Frequently people felt free to make rude, insulting remarks about Lancelot.

"What a long dog! Who stretched him out!"

"Let's put mustard on 'im and have 'im for lunch."

Every time someone said something mean and stupid about Lancelot, I always bent down to tell him that to me he was a very fine, intelligent dog and a good friend, and at this he would wag his tail and look at me with his sad brown eyes.

If only I could, I'd have let him loose and free. If I did that, would he return to Miss Hornby of his own volition? Stern as she was, still I think she truly loved Lancelot and undoubtedly told him secrets that nobody else knew; it is possible that he loved her too. I kept him on his leash, as she ordered, but I always let Lancelot stop to say hello and get acquainted with any other dog who might be out for a walk. Dogs must long to see other dogs; perhaps they get as lonely as people.

Twice as I led Lancelot through the park, I passed the girl who looked like Tanja. She always sat at the same bench, where she smoked, listened to a transistor radio and gazed idly at the Bay. She noticed me, I'm sure, but never smiled or said hello.

And so I walked on. Although it was the money I thought I wanted as I walked the dogs, I hadn't realized I would become so attached to my new friends, Budi and Lancelot.

The telephone rang one evening as we were having dinner. My second call.

"Good evening, may I please speak wih Danica? I'm not sure how to pronounce the name!"

The voice was so musical and rich, I knew it must be an actress or singer who called. And to think she had the kindness to want to pronounce my name correctly! I told her. "This is Danica Pavelic."

"I saw your ad in the paper. I'm desperately in need of someone to walk my dog, Skira. Can you come and talk with me about it? Let's see, how about tomorrow at five?"

"I'll be happy to come."

My voice was subdued but I could not hide the excitement at the thought of meeting Miss Vivienne Marsh.

Everything having to do with her would have to be perfect to match that remarkable voice. She lived where I expected she would live, in my favorite tower, The Barcelona, a tall white building that overlooked the Bay. I had often admired the tiled fountain and formal garden at the entrance to the tower. Now I was admitted to the foyer and rode the elevator to the penthouse at the very top of the building. A small maid met me at the door and invited me to wait in the living room. I was overwhelmed by the sensation of light that filled this tall room, the ivory satin tones of the walls and the bone-white, thick rug on the floor. A curved sofa of apricot-colored velvet accented the lightness of the room, and behind it was placed an enormous brilliant painting in a massive gold frame.

As I stood admiring the painting, I was suddenly aware that I was not alone, and turning around I saw Skira, certainly the most beautiful dog I've ever seen and the most unusual. A tall slender dog, she was covered with a long, silky, tawny coat of hair. Her tail curved up and around, like a monkey's tail. She stood erect and alert, regarding me with golden eyes. It was clear that she was a royal dog, one such as kings and queens would keep. And so I was complimented when this proud beast walked over to me in her poised aristocratic way and let me pet her.

"Ah! I see that Skira has chosen to become friends with you. What an honor for you, Danica! She doesn't take to everyone. How are you, my dear? I'm so glad you could come."

Miss Vivienne Marsh stood in the doorway as she spoke and then moved gracefully across the room, her hands outstretched to hold mine in greeting. She was as lovely a woman as Skira was unique as a dog. Her hair was long, tawny and silky, her eyes a deep violet blue, and though she was not young . . . perhaps thirty or forty . . . she moved with a lithe grace. We sat together on the sofa and I could not take my eyes from her. I memorized the details of her creamy silk housecoat so I could tell Mirjana about it. I may have wanted to look like my cousin Marija before, but now I wished with all my heart that I were Vivienne Marsh.

"I was glad to read your ad, Danica, because I'm looking for someone who can exercise Skira in the late afternoon. I jog each morning in the park and she comes with me, but at this time of day I'm due at the theater."

So she must be an actress!

"If you and Skira like one another, then both of us would more than appreciate it if you could find some time for her. She really seems to have taken to you. Do animals always like you so readily?"

"It seems that way. I like them very much." I floundered, thinking I should say something more. "I should like very much . . ."

My English left me completely and I could not finish the sentence. Tactfully, Miss Marsh nodded and explained.

"You see Skira is a young, sensitive dog and it's hard on her to be kept in an apartment all day. She's been raised in the country where she's been allowed to run freely. Weekends I get out when I can so that she has the freedom to run. How she loves it! Afghans are among the fastest dogs, you know. Unfortunately, we cannot let her run loose in the city, although she may try to break away and do just that. I hope you're strong."

"Oh yes, very strong. I've never seen a dog like this, Miss Marsh."

"You haven't? Well, Skira is an Afghan, and there are

many stories about the breed, which is very old. Some people even say that Noah took an afghan in the ark with him! That's just a story. But pictures of these dogs have appeared in paintings in Greece and in Egypt 6000 years B.C. How the afghan ever got to Afghanistan, nobody knows. It's a wild, hilly country there and the dogs are strong and able to scramble over the hills. Poor Skira! She was born here but I think she longs for her native country."

So Skira was a foreigner too, like me. Now I was sure we would understand one another.

"Would you like to take her out now and see how you get along?" Miss Marsh asked. "When you come back we can make arrangements."

"All right," I said, taking the leash. Skira came with me willingly. We walked through the park and I pretended I was Miss Marsh.

"Skira, Skira!" I called, imitating the actress' low, throaty voice. Skira turned around in surprise, and if dogs could laugh, she would have doubled over howling. She strode on in her aristocratic style, as if she were above all other creatures, including human beings. Once, however, she rushed at a flock of pigeons who were waddling around in the grass for the sheer pleasure of scaring them into flight, and with that I knew she was in some ways like any ordinary mutt.

Perhaps I stood straighter, perhaps I felt taller and prouder because I held the leash of this elegant dog. To have met Skira and Miss Marsh would have been excitement enough for one day, but there was still another surprise in store. The girl who resembled Tanja sat on her usual bench where she gazed into the distance. She wore a slouch-brimmed hat of red felt and a tightly buckled raincoat that went all the way to the ground. Although she had never spoken to me before, the sight of Skira loosened her tongue.

"Is that your dog?" she asked as though she couldn't believe it. "It's beautiful."

"Thanks," I said, not explaining that I didn't own Skira. I lingered for a moment now that I could look at the girl without seeming to stare. It was clear she was not really like Tanja at all, lacking her rosy-cheeked good health and lively brown eyes. Her forehead curved in the same way and there was something in the line of her cheek that was like Tanja's, yet this was a different girl entirely. Stringy brown hair, slanted green eyes and a paleness about her made her less attractive than she could have been, and yet there was a pertness in her smile that I liked.

"Want to sit down?" she asked.

"Sorry. I can't. Not now. Maybe tomorrow?"

"If I'm here," the girl said indifferently, crushing the butt of her cigarette. "Maybe I will and maybe I won't."

"I hope you will be," I said. She glanced at me sharply. Perhaps she noticed my accent for the first time. Would it matter to her, I wondered, would she mind? Would she make fun of me the way some children did, imitating me?

"Good-bye," I said as Skira tugged at the leash.

"See ya," she said casually, as though it didn't matter much one way or the other.

Miss Marsh was delighted that Skira and I got along so well, and we made arrangements for me to take Skira each afternoon when I finished Budi and Lancelot. I could have sung for happiness, so much did I adore Skira, admire Miss Vivienne Marsh and wonder about the girl who looked like Tanja.

As I went home, I could feel that the air was full of promises.

CHAPTER 18

If the girl who looked like Tanja did not wait for me the next day, I could hardly have blamed her, for a sudden chilly rain poured out of the sky.

"Such awful weather, such a rainy day!" Mrs. Weiss cried, clasping her tiny hands. "But Budi must go out for a few minutes only and then come right back. He musn't catch cold."

She finished buckling the smart red and green plaid wool coat that was tailored just for him, and then she stopped in surprise.

"Where's your hat, Danica? Your umbrella?"

"I don't bother with them," I shrugged off her question. I didn't own an umbrella and I detested my old-country cap. Mrs. Weiss insisted on tying a kerchief around my head and placing an umbrella in my hand. So Budi and I took a quick walk to the park but did not see the new Tanja and then we dashed home.

"Just the day for a cup of tea," Mrs. Weiss said as she greeted us, "and Budi, you may have a treat too."

She placed two dog biscuits on a china plate on the floor. As I looked through the window and admired a seaplane that flew in front of the dark blue mountain range,

Dr. Weiss stood beside me. "Lovely isn't it, like a big bird?"

He led me to the round coffee table on which a pale pink linen cloth had been laid for the tea, along with a porcelain teapot, small fluted cups, a plate of round cookies with jam centers and three linen napkins, everything delicate and fine. As Mrs. Weiss poured the tea, Dr. Weiss asked where my family came from, why we had come here and how we were getting along.

"Ernest is dying of curiosity," Mrs. Weiss said, but I did not mind and answered his questions. Timidly I asked Dr. Weiss if he had been here a long time.

"Ach yes, a very long time. By coming here, we cheated the Nazis out of a few victims, but then, Danica, I wouldn't expect you would know about that."

"But I do, Dr. Weiss," I assured him. "My father was a fighter even though he was very young. There were always enemies trying to overcome us. The Nazis, the Italians, the Russians. There was always fighting. He told me about it many times."

"Yes, yes," said Mrs. Weiss, "but that's all over now. We must not look back, but ahead to the future, and most of all we must enjoy the present. Will you have another cookie, Danica?"

I took another buttery morsel and wished Mama could taste it. She baked very well, but differently.

"To the future," Dr. Weiss said, holding up his teacup as though he were making a toast. "If I could read tea leaves, I'd read Danica's future. Because, little Danica, I think you have one. Don't ask me how I know. It is something about which I have an intuition. So tell me, what will you do with your life?"

Everything stopped as I heard the same words my father had used. A vision of Vesna crossed my mind,

Vesna telling me I had the gift and I must not waste it; and yet I had forgotten Vesna, forgotten my ambition and worst of all I had not remembered at all or even thought of the vow I had made to my father.

I began to speak, but could not get the words out. Here was a genuine doctor, a well-known doctor. How could I, an immigrant, a country girl who could not even speak English well, tell him that I too expected to be a doctor? Besides, as Mirjana had said and as I very well knew, coming to Canada had changed me.

Mrs. Weiss came to my rescue.

"Now leave her alone, Ernest, she's only thirteen. It's too early for her to know what she wants to become."

"H'm, but it's good to have a direction," Dr. Weiss said, "and I think Danica has some thoughts but she isn't telling us about them yet. It's all right, Danica, wait until you are ready. In the meanwhile, more tea?"

"Ernest, maybe you'll play the piano for us?"

"I would like to if Danica can stay . . ."

"A little while only," I said apologetically and explained that Miss Hornby would give me "misdemeanors" if I were late again. The Weisses did not know what that meant, and when I told them they were shocked. "Such militaristic methods!"

Gentle people, kind people, lonely people! I knew that the Weisses were my friends. If I weren't so shy, I'd have kissed them both.

The clock struck and Mrs. Weiss insisted I borrow the umbrella and Dr. Weiss promised he would play a little Mozart for me some other time.

CHAPTER 19

Despite my resolves about making comparisons, I could not help thinking that in Kalovar May was a month of sunshine and flowers. Here day after day after day the sun took a long vacation and did not bother to show up. The city became gray and colorless. As I walked the dogs I looked for the girl who made me think of Tanja, but the bench where I had seen her was empty.

Our tiny basement apartment became darker and smaller, and even Mirjana's vivid bouquets of paper flowers failed to cheer it up. Each day Mama came home worn out. Sometimes I caught her sitting at the table with paper and pencil trying to figure out how to pay for everything, but when Mirjana asked, "Mamo, let me help you," she only said, "It's nothing, nothing," and crumpled the paper.

Nor was everything going as smoothly for Marko as he would have us believe. Sometimes he came home from school with bruises on his cheeks or a tear in his jacket or pants.

"You're fighting, Marko. What's the matter with you? What do you have to fight about?" Mama would ask. "You never fought before."

Marko never told us about the scraps at school, but I suspect that someone made fun of him and he would not stand for it. He was proud, like my father.

Only Mirjana carried on with good-natured cheery words of encouragement for everyone, as though in a little while the sun would come out and everything would be all right for all of us. Then one gloomy day when I had just come from Miss Vivienne's suite, there was Mirjana sitting quietly in the living room. Immediately I sensed that something was wrong. All right, Danica, I thought, time to cheer her up a little.

"Listen, Mirjana, I have just become Miss Vivienne Marsh. Watch me!"

I floated into the room and stood languid and graceful as I repeated the words my employer had spoken less than an hour ago. "Danica, when you take Skira out this week, please be sure that she does not become involved with any other dogs. I hear there's a vicious hound loose in the park. We wouldn't want Skira attacked, so do be careful."

I hoped they would think I was trying to be funny, although I really did want to talk like Miss Marsh. But Marko snorted, rolled his eyes and imitated me.

"Brat!" I made a face at him.

My mother stood at the kitchen door. "Do you have a cold, Danica? You're talking through your nose. Must be this terrible weather."

From the depths of her chair, Mirjana commented at last. "Danica, you don't sound quite like an English actress. Better speak natural."

"Spik natural!" I echoed her, emphasizing her accent, which was ridiculous because Mirjana spoke better than the rest of us.

"You are a perfect English actress, I suppose," I said, throwing a pillow at Mirjana, to try to stir her out of her gloom. At any other time Mirjana would have thrown the pillow back at me, chased me, tickled me, and we would have ended up getting silly and having fun. But now she only put the pillow away and sighed as if I were nothing more than a troublesome child.

"Come on, Mir," I said, "you were more fun in Kalovar. You wouldn't let me get away with that there."

"It's time you grew up a little," she said, more to end the conversation than anything else. Tears glimmered in her eyes and suddenly she rushed into the bedroom, slamming the door behind her.

"Mamo, what's that all about?"

"I don't know. She got a letter from her girl friend, Ana."

"Bad news?"

"She wouldn't tell me what it said." Mama shrugged her shoulders helplessly. When Mirjana decided not to talk, nothing would move her to change her mind. I talked to Mirjana through the bedroom door.

"Hey, Mir, I didn't mean to hurt your feelings. I was only kidding. Anyway, you speak better than any of us. I'm sorry, all right?"

Sniffles from the bedroom.

"Did something happen, Mirjana? You can tell me. I'm a good listener."

Silence.

"Mirjana, you can *trust* me. I'm on your side. I'd understand."

"Go away, Danica. Leave me alone."

I left her alone as she asked. Something was not right. Just as something upset Mama, as Marko bore his battles alone, Mirjana too was being hurt. Nor was I brimming over with happiness. For the first time I wondered if it had been a terrible mistake for us to come.

CHAPTER 20

The sun came back, golden and smiling, as though it had never abandoned us. One day we were wearing winter coats and the next we peeled them off and could not bear to stay inside. Streets, parks, front yards, balconies and beaches were filled with people of all ages lying out flat or sitting on benches and holding their faces up to the sun, waiting for its blessing. Many wore bathing suits, the skimpiest of bikinis and the briefest of covering as they lay in their front yards or even in empty lots and public parks. Mama was horrified.

"It is shameful, sinful," she gasped. "Why, they are almost naked and some of the worst ones are older men and women too. Mirjana, Danica, Marko, if I ever catch you . . ."

She did not have to worry. We pretended to be sophisticated about this sudden blooming of near nudity, yet it made us uncomfortable too. Anyway, the weather turned chilly again and so I was back to my ugly brown coat. Even Budi was wearing his tartan coat when I went to call for him.

We walked in the park as usual, and suddenly the day brightened as I saw the new Tanja. I had not seen her for almost two weeks and gave up the thought of meeting her again, but there she was, in a long, faded cotton skirt and a floppy straw hat, just as though it were a hot day in the middle of summer. Only an incongruous rust-colored sweater jarred the picture she made as she sat there smoking, a discontented expression on her face.

"Going somewhere?" she asked as I walked toward her bench.

"Out for a walk."

"A different dog today. Just how many dogs do you have?"

"None. It's a job I have. I walk dogs for people who don't have the time. But I can't stand around. The dogs have to get their exercise. Want to walk with me?"

She crushed her cigarette slowly, thought about it for several seconds, then stood up languidly. "All right. I suppose so."

We walked along a path under giant cedar trees.

"Lucky you, having a job," she said. "Wish I did."

"Why don't you look for one?"

"Are you kiddin'? I mean, a real job. How much do you make?"

I shrugged my shoulders, not wanting to tell her. She understood and did not get angry.

"One like this wouldn't even buy my smokes. I don't work for peanuts."

"Peanuts? I don't get peanuts. I get money," I said puzzled, and then I was ashamed when she laughed. The English language uses too many phrases that aren't in the dictionary. I smiled apologetically.

"To work for peanuts means you don't get rich on a job. Anyway, I'm not so sure I want to work. My mom's got a job and she gets awfully bored."

"My mother works too," I said, glad we had something in common. "Does your father work?"

"Who has fathers these days?" she said. "Mine skipped off when I was two, the rat, so Mom had me on her hands. Only now she's getting tired and she's after me all the time to find work. I'm not in that much of a hurry."

I didn't know what to say. Even in Kalovar sometimes, though certainly not often, a man runs away from his wife and child. My father could never have done such a thing, nor could I imagine Mama "getting tired" of us.

"You're foreign, aren't you?" she asked. "Where are you from?"

"Kalovar. It's a little town in Croatia. I guess you never heard of Kalovar."

"Are you kidding? I never even heard of Croatia, wherever that is."

"You never heard of *Croatia?*" This girl shocked me with every statement she made. "You've heard of Yugoslavia, haven't you?"

"Sort of."

I picked up a stick and drew a map in the dirt. "Here's Italy coming down into the Mediterranean, and then to the east there's more land. Here's Greece down here; Albania is above it; and all this land here is Yugoslavia. This part here is Croatia and here's Zagreb, the capital."

"Of Yugoslavia or Croatia? You're mixing me up."

This girl was certainly ignorant, but perhaps she could not be expected to know of a country so far away. "Yugoslavia is made up of many small countries and each one has a different culture, different language, even different churches. There's Croatia, Serbia which is here, Macedonia, Slovenia, Montenegro and Hercegovina. But it's not like the provinces in Canada or the states in the United States, because each country has a special history. There isn't even a Yugoslav language. The history . . ."

I could have gone on explaining all this because certainly she should be acquainted with what to me was such common knowledge, but she was smiling in a superior way and not really listening.

"You're a very funny girl. Are you always so serious? It's cute. How old are you?"

I pretended not to understand. If I told her I was only thirteen, she might not want to have anything to do with me. "How old?" I asked as if I wasn't sure what she meant. "How old are you?"

"Seventeen."

"I'm sixteen," I answered, glad I was tall enough to get away with it. At least she seemed to believe me.

"What's your name?"

"Danica Pavelic."

"Wha-a-at? That's a mouthful. Say it slow."

I repeated it and asked her her name.

"Audrey Lewis. Look, Don, whatever it is, your name is pretty weird. Why don't we call you Donna or Donny for short?"

"It's not my name. It wouldn't be right."

"Sure it would. You want to sound Canadian, don't you?"

"Yes, but . . . well, I couldn't change my *name*." For all that I wanted so much to be completely Canadian, at the first test I chose to remain myself, Danica. "My father named me so I can't change it. Danica means Morning Star. I don't want to be Donny or anything like that."

Audrey tossed her head. "Up to you. Some people like being foreigners." It was clear she was glad she wasn't one, and she was miffed because I didn't agree with her.

"I really want to be Canadian," I said. I was remembering how my father used to talk with me, loving my name. Danica, Danica! His voice was full of love, as though this were the most beautiful name in the world, and this was why he gave it to me. No, I would never change it.

Audrey changed the subject. "You got a boyfriend, Donna?"

If she planned to be that persistent, perhaps we wouldn't be friends after all, I was thinking. Yet she looked at me in a friendly way and again I was reminded of Tanja. I wanted a friend my own age more than anything else. Perhaps later she would learn to call me by my name.

"No, I don't have one," I told her. In Kalovar we didn't even think about "boyfriends" until we were seventeen or so. "And you, Audrey?"

"I had one, the rat, He walked out on me, so now I'm free. Maybe we can find some boys, you and me. We could have fun."

I didn't know how to answer that! Certainly, even if I wanted to "find some boys," Mama would have something to say about that. I hoped that Audrey wouldn't keep talking about it. We were walking along the road that led to some gardens. Birds darted back and forth in the tall cypress trees overhead, Budi trotted in front of us, and for a while we walked quietly, saying nothing. Then Audrey began to sing a popular song, one I think I'd heard on television. Her voice was surprisingly sweet, thin perhaps, certainly not as full and rich as Tanja's, and yet there was a delicacy in the way she sang that I wouldn't have expected. We walked on and then she began another song and this was one I knew, so I harmonized with her. It reminded me of the times Tanja and I used to listen to the radio to learn the new songs. When we finished, Audrey rewarded me with a spontaneous smile.

"Not bad!" she said and asked if I knew a song called "Can't Get You Outta my Mind," but I didn't recall it, I told her, but would like to learn it. At the moment though I had to rush off and take Budi back because Miss Hornby would have a fit if I were late.

She shrugged her shoulders. "I wouldn't hurry for anyone."

"Will you wait for me?" I asked.

"Maybe yes. Maybe no. Think I'll get a cup of coffee."

"Then maybe I'll see you later. All right?"

I said good-bye, not able to tell if Audrey were my friend or not. Miss Hornby wanted me to buy some stamps for her, so Lancelot's walk was confined to Davie Street. But later when I returned to the park with Skira, Audrey was waiting for me, or perhaps it was Skira she wanted to see.

"Hello, pretty thing," she said. "Come over and let Audrey pet you."

Skira looked at her disdainfully and turned her head away.

"Darn you, I said come over here and let me pet you," she said menacingly. Skira tugged gently at the leash and paid no attention.

"Snobby dog!" Audrey said. "Dogs always love me. This is the first one that ever acted so snooty."

"Don't feel bad," I said. "She's fussy. Even Miss Marsh says she is hardly ever friendly."

"Miss Marsh? Which Miss Marsh?" Audrey asked, alert now, turning her slanted green eyes toward me.

"Miss Vivienne Marsh, the actress. She owns her."

Audrey changed, the narrow eyes growing wide. "You mean that Miss Marsh, *the* Vivienne Marsh, the famous actress, lets *you* take out her dog every day?"

"Sure."

"That's something now, isn't it?" she said, whistling in admiration. "You really *know* her?" She became more friendly now, got up and began to walk with me over the green meadow. "How'd you ever manage that? You're really quite a person, Donny. You're not even here three months and you know Vivienne Marsh."

"It just happened, that's all."

"Just happened, that's all!" she said, imitating me. Then she laughed, put her hand on my sleeve and said, "Donny, you know something, I'm beginning to get some fabulous ideas for both of us. For you and for me!"

"What ideas? What are you talking about?"

"You'll see in time," she said. At least something was making her happy. As we walked along the brook that led to the lake, she began to sing and invited me to join her. She taught me the words and music of two songs that afternoon, and then I had to take Skira back.

CHAPTER 21

At last I had a friend. Nobody could have been less like Tanja, my dreamy friend in Kalovar who embroidered a sentimental design on a kerchief for me and told fortunes by picking petals off daisies, than Audrey. Now I was beginning to realize just how good a friend Tanja had been, always there when I wanted her, forever kind, willing to scramble up the mountainside with me for a picnic, or walk with me, arm in arm on Sundays when everyone paraded along the main street of the town.

With Audrey it was different. Each time I met her, I could not be sure but what it would be the last time. When she opened her mouth to speak, I couldn't tell whether she would make fun of my accent or tell me how astounding it was that I should be here but a few months and yet have a business of my own.

"Don't you want to work at all? I mean, don't you get bored all day with nothing to do?" I asked her.

"One of these days I'll surprise you. Remember, Donny, I told you, I got ideas, ideas for both of us!"

But what those ideas were, she would not tell. It annoyed me a little to see that she enjoyed making me curious.

Still, she waited for me almost every day. It did not take me long to discover that it wasn't I who fascinated her but my employer.

"Tell me," she would say as we walked along the lake known as the Lost Lagoon, while I restrained Budi from chasing the proud Canadian geese into the water, "what is Vivienne Marsh really like?"

"She's nice," was all I could say.

"Nice, nice! *Tell* me about her!" Audrey cried. The mention of her name, Vivienne Marsh, set off a certain excitement in Audrey so that her green eyes widened as she asked me all sorts of silly questions; what does she wear, does she dye her hair, are there men around her apartment, does she have big cocktail parties, does she ever get a little high?

"For heaven's sake, Audrey, I call for Skira and bring her back. That is all. I don't know all those personal things about her."

Even if I did, I could not possibly tell Audrey about them. Vivienne Marsh was the loveliest woman I had ever seen in all my life. Perhaps I worshiped her. I did not mean to cry in exasperation at Audrey's questions and I was sorry if I sounded short-tempered, but I could not talk of Miss Marsh to her.

She took this rebuke in good spirits and asked no more questions.

"Come, Skira, come say hello to Audrey," she begged in a sickeningly sweet voice, but when Skira turned her noble head away from Audrey, she became despondent. "Even that dog thinks she's too good for me," she said.

Then I had to comfort poor Audrey in her ratty white sweater and drooping straw hat. "Let's sing 'Last night,' " I begged. "I never can remember the words."

And so she began to sing and I harmonized, being care-

ful not to let my voice get too strong, and soon Audrey
was in a good humor again.

"I'll have to take you in hand, make a Canadian out of
you," she said one day as we walked together along the
seawall.

"It's exactly what I want to be," I said. "A Canadian."

"First lesson," she said, lighting a cigarette and placing
it between my lips. "There, breathe in now. You'll see
how good it is."

I didn't want it, but she held it firmly, and having no
choice, I breathed in, choked, coughed and felt unclean.
"Not for me, Audrey. Anyway, I could have done this in
Croatia, nothing particularly Canadian about it."

"You don't know what you're missing. But it don't
matter."

She liked to think she shocked me. How innocent we
must have seemed, two girls strolling through the park
with a dog at the end of a leash, both of us stopping to
admire the new ducklings that swam behind their mother
in the pond or to watch the childen as they scrambled
over the rings and bars of the playground. Yet all the time
Audrey was telling me stories about what "really went
on" in the West End and at school, watching with her
bright green eyes to see my shocked reaction at each new
tale of drugs or prostitution or shocking crimes. It could
not have been difficult to shock me.

"I don't know how people can do such things, Audrey,
do you?"

"What a prude you are! You just haven't been around.
Let me tell you about this party I went to once. Everyone
was drunk and there were twelve people standing on one
of those balconies on the fourteenth floor and throwing
beer bottles down into the street . . ."

"And then what happened?"

Audrey's eyes flashed with a knowing smile every time I asked. What a good storyteller she was! Even though I suspected that most of the stories she told me weren't even true, still I was fascinated, a bird hypnotized by a snake. Every time I asked that question, "And then what happened?" Audrey smiled, as if she held me in her power.

"Your clothes are really awful," she said one day. "Haven't you got anything else?"

"What a nice way to begin a conversation," I said sarcastically, but she was right. My clothes from Kalovar embarrassed me, making me look too young and very countrified. All I had been able to buy after long hours of dog walking was one pair of jeans and a shirt.

"Listen, Donny, I'll let you in on something good," Audrey said, winking, as though she were doing me a favor. "You can get clothes like mine, real cheap. Only you mustn't tell anyone else."

Clothes like Audrey's? She wore her new skirt with its maroon and orange stripes, topped with a gauzy blouse cut much too low, with a kind of exciting flare. Mama would have been horrified at such an outfit and insisted that only the worst kind of girl would wear such clothes. It was clear they would never do for me. I thanked Audrey but mumbled that I could not go.

"Okay, if you *want* to look like a hick . . ." she said.

How I wanted something new, anything to keep me from looking so drab! But it was Miss Marsh, not Audrey, who would be my guide.

Alone, I wandered downtown to an exclusive store, the kind that Miss Marsh would consider suitable. Even, the junior dresses were beyond my savings, but I dallied among the counters where treasures of perfumes and cosmetics were sold. There I bought a stick of blue paint for my eyelids, mascara and a small pot of lip rouge. At home I locked myself in the bathroom and practiced putting on the makeup so that it would appear subtly shining like Miss Marsh's and not crudely painted like Audrey's, but I only ended up looking like a child with colors on her face. When I could not get off all the eye shadow, Mama asked if there was something wrong, my eyes were so hollow, and she insisted I wasn't getting enough sleep.

I was getting to know Audrey, to understand her moods of depression, the way she would ridicule my accent or insist that I sang too loud when we sang together, though she would get angry if I stopped to listen to her. On the other hand, she was unexpectedly kind, truly helped me with my English even though I recognized grammatical errors in her speech, and for the most part it was pleasant to walk with her in the afternoon. Sometimes I treated her to an ice cream cone; she insisted on buying me coffee. I liked my new friend, but she was rakish, odd and not always nice. And I had no other friend.

Only once did I lose patience with her.

"I'd like to see some of your employers. That Dr. Weiss, or the old school mistress . . ."

It was clear she did not care about them, but was leading up to an invitation to see Miss Marsh. I said nothing. She went on.

"It wouldn't hurt you just to show me where Miss Marsh lives. I could wait outside for you, or downstairs in the lobby."

I stopped short. "Audrey, you must never never come

with me or wait for me or anything like that. I mean it."

"Well, don't get so mad about it. Why shouldn't I?"

But I couldn't tell her that with her smudgy makeup, stringy brown hair and dirty blouse so sheer that I could see she wore nothing under it, I didn't want anyone, particularly Miss Marsh, to think she was my friend. It wasn't kind of me but it was the truth, a truth I could not tell her.

"Audrey, I don't want to lose my job. They'll think I'm not serious about it if you wait for me. You mustn't come. Do you understand?"

She understood all right. The green eyes flashed defiantly, but she kept back the acid words she wanted to throw in my face.

"It's okay," she said in a low, meek voice. I felt ashamed of what I'd been thinking, yet I didn't take back my words. Instead I put my arms around her, this troubled and troublesome friend of mine.

CHAPTER 22

The weather changed dramatically. The sweet, dreamy beginnings of summer turned to a cold, frequently rainy dullness in which everything was reduced to a fog so gray that the mountains to the north, which were usually so startling a blue, disappeared entirely.

Audrey disappeared as well. A summer friend, my father would have called her, one who comes out only when the sun is shining. Once she had told me that when the weather was bad, she liked to stay in bed all day. But could she do this for two weeks?

So I walked through the park alone with the dogs. Other matters brought a frown to my forehead so deep that Mrs. Weiss asked me what was wrong and I said, "Why, nothing!" hastily.

Actually this new country seemed to be giving each one of us secret sorrows such as we never had before, problems we could not easily confide because we did not quite understand them. We felt each other blundering along and somehow tried to be helpful without prying.

Mirjana and I were upset by the vague fear and worry that we read in Mama's face when she thought we weren't watching her. One night she wrote a page of figures with some difficulty, and when we asked her what it was all about, she covered up the figures quickly and said it was only homework. Mirjana looked up from the paper flowers she was fashioning. At least they were selling well.

"Mamo, I've been thinking about the restaurant . . ." Mirjana would begin in an effort to encourage Mama. "With ten thousand Croatians in this city and thousands more people who like good food, the only problem we're going to have is finding a place big enough."

"Sure, sure," Mama answered, not impressed, not comforted.

But Mirjana talked enthusiastically about the new project as if it were already a fact. She had us all arguing for a week about the name of the restaurant, and when we finally decided on The New Zagreb, the place almost seemed to exist. Mirjana kept coming up with ideas for decorating the restaurant.

"Along one wall we'll have a platform with five or six tables and a thatched roof like we had at home, to suggest an outdoor courtyard. We can tie on grapevines, leaves and bunches of grapes, so it will be like the Inn."

"Fine!" I said sarcastically, "and where will you find grapes that grow indoors?"

"Not real ones, honey," Mirjana answered, ignoring my cynicism. "We'll use artificial ones made of plastic or paper, and we can all make leaves. It will suggest a grape arbor. Then, the walls on the other side will be covered with murals of folk dancers. We'll use woven tablecloths like we did at home. And of course there'll be music, records or tapes; sometimes we can have live musicians. And the waitresses will wear embroidered blouses and longish skirts, like at home."

"It's all so very folksy and sweet," I said, taunting her. Actually, it was a good idea, only I wanted to wear modern clothes when I waited on tables there.

"In summer we can put some of the tables outdoors,

and have plants in tubs, so it's like a garden," Mirjana went on, "and wait till you see how much money you make in tips, Danica. Then you won't have to walk your dogs any more."

"But I like my dogs. I don't want to give up my jobs."

"Come now, no need to worry about it *yet,*" Mama said. "Not for a long time."

The idea of making money in tips appealed to me. Best of all, when Mirjana and Mama talked about the restaurant with one inspired idea leaping up after another, their faces began to shine with anticipation and for a while they seemed to forget their problems, whatever they might be.

However, even though we sometimes stayed up later than we should to dream of The New Zagreb, Mirjana always ended with a word of warning. "Don't forget, Mamo. Once the restaurant is under way, I'm going back to Kalovar."

Then the idea of the restaurant hovered in the air while we went back to our private realities. Mama said, "I understand," to Mirjana's reservation, but as she got up, I heard her say under her breath, "Maybe she'll go back, and maybe not." She shook her head sadly and went to bed.

It was a frightening thing to see my mother lose confidence, and though we said nothing, we were unsettled to find this happening to Mama. I could think of nothing else, so after school one day and before I had to walk the dogs, I went to the back door of the restaurant where Mama worked. I saw her stir seasoning into a heavy pot and then lift another large restaurant pan and carry it to the counter. For the first time it seemed to me that she looked older and more tired than usual. The men who worked in the kitchen, waiters, dishwashers, busboys and another chef, moved silently, an unfriendly crew. One of them began to say something to Mama but another one jostled his arm and nodded his head toward me as if to say, "Be quiet; her daughter is sitting right there." Poor Mama, it was not easy for men to see a woman work as chef, particularly one who could hardly speak English.

When Mama saw me, she came over and kissed me. "Is everything all right, Danica? I didn't expect you here."

"Everything's fine. Mamo, I'm going to treat you to some coffee."

"You treat me? Silly girl. There's coffee here."

"No, Mamo. We're going to sit down and be waited on like other people. So come on."

"If you say so. . . ." Mamo took off her apron, patted her hair into shape and put on her coat, smiling all the time, so she must have been pleased.

Not far from the Villa Rosanna was a small, neat bakery that always sent out the delicious fragrance of newly baked breads and cakes. It was here that I stood in line many times to get bread from the pretty, yellow-haired young woman who always asked in the old-country way, "Yes, Madam?" even though we had become acquainted and she knew my name. She stood in a straight, dignified manner, like a queen in her palace.

Mama and I sat at one of the small tables, and she came over to us with a smiling, "Yes, Madam?" I ordered coffee and the delicious raspberry tarts Mama adored.

"It's nice, being out with you," Mama said, pleased at this unexpected treat though she objected when I insisted on paying for it. "What did you want to talk about? Something special?"

"Later. I want to know what you think of this place."

Mama noticed the colorful peasant decorations on the

wall, the order and cleanliness of the shop, the long line of people waiting in front of the counter, and the greedy way everyone's eyes followed the baker as he came from the kitchen bearing a tray full of perfectly formed strawberry tarts. He was a tall man with a mustache, a proud man, who reminded me a little of my father.

When we left the shop, Mama insisting first on buying some of the strawberry tarts for dinner, I asked again what she thought of the bakery.

"A very good place. Good quality. Good business and nice people."

"That's what I hoped you would say, Mamo. You see the pretty girl and her husband, the baker, have been here for six years, that's all; they came over from Europe, like us, and yet they have a good place of their own. So you see, it can be done!"

"*Oj,* Danica," Mama laughed and pinched my cheek as if I were five years old instead of practically an adult. "You're a good girl to try to give me courage. Thank you. I shall always remember."

It was good to see that my treat pleased her. She walked more lightly and erectly all the way home. I would even have said she seemed hopeful.

Later that day, as I entered the apartment after having walked the dogs, I heard great sobs of grief from the bedroom where Mirjana lay, no longer caring who heard her loud weeping.

"For heaven's sake, what's it all about, Mamo? What's going on?"

Mama, upset and distracted, stirred the soup, then sliced the bread, picked up her knitting and dropped it again. "You might as well know, Danica. She's been getting letters saying that Mirko has been seeing her friend, Ana."

"Ana's her best friend. So?"

"That's what makes it hard. Today Ana wrote to say that she and Mirko will be getting married soon."

"Oh no! That's terrible. He promised to wait."

"Ha! Since when can you trust a man to wait? I would have trusted your father, yes. But not most men. In a way I can't blame Mirko; a man cannot wait forever."

I buttered a slice of my mother's good bread and bit into it, while the sobs vibrated through the apartment. "Mirjana's silly. Once you see Vancouver, how can you even think of going back?"

"I know, Danica. I'll confess at first I wanted to go back, but even though it's not that easy here, still I want to stay."

"It's not as if Mirko were the only man in the world."

"But Mirjana is in love. She is not sensible like you."

"Besides," I went on, "what's so good about marriage? Nowadays a man and a woman can simply live together and then split when they're tired of each other." I was showing off what Audrey had told me, but it was the last straw where Mama was concerned. If she was upset with Mirjana, she was furious with me.

"What kind of talk is this? What's happening to you to ask, 'What's so good about marriage?' It is the right thing, the best thing in the world a girl can do, to be married." She drew her breath in sharply and it was clear she was so angry that her head shook. "To live with a man and not be married is a sin, a shameful thing to do, a terrible mistake. Besides, it's stupid. The woman always gets the worst of it. What can be better than to be married?"

To be Canadian, I was thinking, to be modern like Miss Vivienne Marsh. She seemed lighter and happier than anyone I knew, yet she wasn't married. But as a new series of sobs came from the bedroom, Mama was too unhappy to argue with me anymore. Besides, she was making

Mirjana's favorite pudding, a creamy dessert filled with figs and nuts.

Mirjana came to dinner with red eyes and a box of Kleenex. We were all careful not to mention Kalovar, Mirko or anything that would set her off in another torrent of tears. She ate her soup mechanically, but perked up in spite of herself at the pudding and even asked for a second helping.

Mama gave it to her, greatly relieved. A girl who would take two helpings of this rich concoction was not likely to drown herself in the Bay or jump from the top of one of the towers.

But their troubles seemed simple compared to mine. Marko had to fight because someone called him a name, but sooner or later that would be over; he had at least ten good friends already. As for Mirjana, I did not think it such a tragedy if she didn't go back to Kalovar. Once she and Mama started the restaurant, they would both be satisfied. But my troubles were vague, something I could not explain, a feeling of being nowhere, not in Kalovar, not here. I did not want to be a country girl from a small Croatian village, and yet I was not a Canadian. I had no friends except Audrey and I wasn't sure she really liked me. My clothes were all wrong and the money I earned did not go far enough to buy the things I wanted. And my dream of becoming a doctor now appeared so impossible that I set it aside as only a silly notion I had long ago.

On a drizzling Friday afternoon I walked disconsolately with the dogs, huddled up in my old coat and feeling sorry for myself. At last I brought Skira back to the suite. Usually Miss Marsh would have left for the theater and Bella, the maid, would take Skira, but on that day Miss Marsh herself came to the door.

"Hello, Danica! This dreadful weather! You're damp; you must be chilled to the bone. Would you like to come in and get warm? Perhaps we can have a cup of tea together."

She insisted on taking my coat and led me to the fireplace where a fire crackled cheerfully. Miss Marsh, dressed in jade green silk lounging pajamas and long, narrow gold sandals, invited me to sit on a stool next to the fire and suggested I take off my wet shoes. She curled up in a chair and said that Bella would bring in the tea things in a minute.

"It's nice to have a chance to get to know you a little," she said. "Ordinarily I'd be at the theater, but suddenly five performers have the flu, so I have a holiday tonight!"

She smiled, but an expression of momentary sadness passed over her face. "And this sudden vacation leaves me quite alone. Can you imagine it?"

"I don't know what to say," I stammered.

"I'm not sure either," she said airily to put me at ease. "But now we can get better acquainted. Tell me, Danica, how are you getting along?"

Bella came in with a tray of tea things and left, while I wondered what I should say. I had to be careful not to sound as though I were complaining.

"Begin at the beginning, would you, Danica, and tell me how you happened to come to Vancouver," Miss Marsh asked, and she seemed so genuinely interested that soon I found myself telling her all about Kalovar, and my father, and Vesna, and Mama's dream of opening a restaurant.

"I'm afraid I talk too much," I said. Everything seemed to have rushed out before I could stop it.

"Not enough!" Miss Marsh said. "Do you know what a very lucky girl you are?"

I gulped. Me, lucky? She didn't know about Marko

coming home from school with a bloody face, or Mama worrying over a page of figures and Mirjana, silly Mirjana, crying out for Mirko every night once she got in bed.

"I'm not lucky like you, Miss Marsh. You are so beautiful and famous. You live in this wonderful place. And you must know hundreds of people."

"That's all true to an extent. It's not quite what it seems to be. My friends are many but they have their own lives. Other people become friendly because they want me to help them, to grant favors or give them something, money or influence. But real love, such as I think must exist in your little family, is priceless, the most valuable thing in the world."

"I never thought of it that way."

She smiled. "It's always that way. Someday you'll know. My audiences love me perhaps in the way of audiences, and the people I work with are good friends, but when I come home each night, I am alone excepting for Skira. And it's to that handsome Skira that I tell my secrets, my dreams, my sad little stories and my little jokes as well."

At the mention of her name, Skira, who lay beside the fire, turned her aristocratic head, and Miss Marsh nodded at her, as though the two of them shared a secret.

"Skira was the gift of a man, a very dear friend, the one person who probably did love me," she said, holding my gaze with her deep violet eyes. Was this man her lover, I wondered, and what had happened to him? A sudden death or an unfortunate marriage to someone else he could not leave? Of course I dared not ask, and I think she might have told me, but the telephone rang and soon Bella came to tell her the call was hers.

I stood up to leave, thinking it was time, and when she came back she took my hands in hers. "It's a compliment that I trust Skira to you. You are a splendid girl, Danica;

150

I knew this as soon as I saw you. If things seem a little difficult or slow, don't get discouraged. You were meant for a good life."

"Thank you, Miss Marsh. Thank you very much," I whispered. "You are very kind."

Very kind? She was an angel. I had been discouraged for a long time. Now, I began to feel the sweetness of hope.

If I weren't so old, I'd have danced all the way home. I looked up at the cold, scudding clouds that moved over the city and I knew without any doubt that in back of them the sun was shining.

CHAPTER 23

The sun shone but did not choose to come out from behind the clouds until the following Tuesday, and with it came Audrey. I had begun to think she had left Vancouver forever, but when Skira and I entered the park on Tuesday, she was waiting for us at her usual place. This time she sported still another new outfit, sailor pants, a pathetic imitation of a peasant blouse and a man's visored cap on her head. It was such a dreadful combination that I almost found it charming. Audrey had to be talented to dress that badly. She walked toward us, her green eyes sparkling and a wide, sunny smile on her piquant little face. She was an impossible sort of friend, entirely undependable, and yet I was delighted to see her.

First she spoke to Skira. "What's the matter, Skira? Don't you know me? Come, Skira, say how-do. Give me your paw."

The imperious Skira focused her golden eyes on three black Canadian geese in the distance and from the deep growl in her throat and the way she strained at the leash, it was easy to see that she only wanted to show those birds her paw! For a brief moment Audrey showed her annoyance, but recovered quickly, grinning at me.

"How are you, Donny? I missed you, you know," she said as though we were the best friends in the world.

"I missed you too. Where did you go all that time?"

"Where didn't I go! It's a long story. When it first began getting cold, I wanted to stay in bed and my mom got really mad. Talk about unreasonable women! You wouldn't say I was lazy, would you?"

"If you stay in bed all day? That's lazy, Audrey," I answered, afraid I'd hurt her feelings, but it was true. Surprisingly enough she nodded, actually agreeing.

"You're right. So I left home. Hitched my way east to Banff and stayed with some friends. Former friends, I should say. It was sunny there; I sat by the lake, I threw in pebbles, one after the other, and I began to think, what did I really want to do with my life?"

It sounded encouraging, this new Audrey! I waited for her to go on but she interrupted her story. "How's your boss, Donny?"

"Which one?"

"Which one do you think? Vivienne Marsh, of course."

"Okay, I guess. Why?" I could have told her about staying for tea but it was a private matter; I could not tell anyone.

"Just wondered, that's all. She's very nice, isn't she?"

"Sure, I told you that. Tell me what you started to say about your life, Audrey."

"Well, I was thinking perhaps there was one thing I could do that would be worthwhile, but I need help. Donny, if you could help me BECOME someone, would you do it?"

"Yes, of course. But you're so mysterious. What could I possibly do for you?"

"One simple thing. Won't take time, won't cost money. Introduce me to Miss Vivienne Marsh."

I stopped short. My mouth actually trembled. "No, I couldn't possibly do that. Why do you want to meet her so much?"

"Because, dear little country girl, I have decided to become a singer. A pop singer, nightclubs and stuff. If someone like your Miss Marsh puts in only one good word for me, I'll have it made. A job in a club or a theater, or maybe in television, who knows?"

"Audrey, Audrey," I could only shake my head in exasperation. There she was pleading, almost begging for an answer, reminding me of a small dog with the too small nose and shining eyes, and the eager smile to encourage my agreement. If only she could sing! Her voice was sweet enough, yet weak and not always in tune.

"I'd like to help you, Audrey, but don't ask me to introduce you to Miss Marsh because I can't. People are always taking advantage of her just like that, and it's not easy for her. I can't do it. Besides I'm not really a friend. I just work for her."

Audrey nodded her head philosophically. "Exactly what I thought you'd say. All right then, Donny, listen to this. *You and I together!* Think of that!"

"What are you talking about?"

"We both sing good. You harmonize all right. We're not bad looking either. We could work up a little act, sing, start out perhaps in a small club. We'd make lots of money, work our way up, even become famous."

"Not me, Audrey. I'm no singer. Sorry."

"Of course you are. You're terrific. We could do it together for a little while. You want to see me get started, don't you?"

"Why don't you just go and try to get a job by yourself?"

"Don't be silly. You need to be recommended. And you got the best recommendation practically in your hands. You tell Miss Marsh your dreams, you want to be a singer. Tell her you've got an act with a friend. She must like you to let you take Skira out, so she'll say she wants to listen to us. We'll show her how good we can be, she'll be impressed, and we'll be on our way!"

"Can't do it, Audrey."

"With the money you make, you'll be able to get lots of good clothes. Maybe you'll even get a car!"

"Forget about me, Audrey. It's really good that you want to work like that, but it's not for me."

"You never been in a nightclub, I'll bet."

"Not really." I remembered how naively I had spelled out Strip-a-rama that first night in Vancouver. "Stay away," my uncle had advised me jokingly.

She stopped talking about it and we walked toward the rose gardens. She began to sing something we had once sung together and after a while I joined her. We passed three Chinese girls who were laughing lightly over something and when they smiled at us, I smiled back, but I wasn't as lighthearted as they.

"Danica," Audrey said, surprising me by saying my name correctly this time. "Will you come to dinner at my house on Saturday? We can tell our mothers we're going to a movie afterward, but we'll go to a nightclub. I just want you to step in for a minute so you can see it's not really bad at all."

I hesitated. "It won't do any good. I can't."

"But I can. Please, Danica, come for my sake. Will you?"

She was pleading. Was I really seeing a new Audrey, a girl who wanted to be more than a lazy, drifting person? I was her friend so I had to help her.

"I think so," I said. "but I'll have to ask Mama first."

If she had made a face at that I wouldn't have been surprised, but she threw her arms around me and I was amazed!

CHAPTER 24

Never before had I lied to Mama or deceived her in any way, because the occasion had never arisen, but now it was clear that the whole truth would get me nowhere. Mama, full of fears in this strange country, would surely hesitate to let me go to dinner at the house of a friend she did not know. It was different with Marko: he was a boy! To confess that we were going to see if we could get into a nightclub afterward would have horrified her. I decided that a half-truth was at least half as good as the whole truth without considering that a half-truth was also a half-lie.

First I "buttered her up," as the expression goes. On Wednesday I made dinner for the family and on Thursday I helped Mama with her English homework, being careful to praise her and tell her how fast she was improving; fortunately this last was sincere, for she was doing very well. As she closed her workbook and picked up her knitting, I broached the dangerous subject.

"Mamo, you remember I told you about my friend, Audrey, the girl I met when I was out walking the dogs?"

"Yes, and so?"

"She lives with her mother and they invited me for dinner Saturday night and the movies afterward."

Instantly my mother put down her knitting and sat up, alert and suspicious.

"Who is this Audrey? What do you know about her?"

"She's a good friend, Mamo. Nice. She helps me with my English."

"Danica, I think maybe not this time. I don't know this girl or her mother. As for movies, too expensive. Three dollar. And sometimes what they show in movies is not proper for a young girl like you."

"Mamo, it's my own money. I earned it. And sometime you can invite Audrey here for dinner. She's never had a good dinner like you make, stuffed cabbage rolls or *duvec*, or *čevapčiči*."

Mama shook her head, unconvinced.

"Please, Mamo, Pul-lease. I never go anywhere and it's so gloomy here with Mirjana crying all the time. It's not like Kalovar where I had Tanja. Audrey's the only friend I have."

She hesitated, weakened and gave in. "First I must meet this girl. Then we'll see."

"Good! I'll phone her right now."

I couldn't say too much to Audrey over the phone with my mother listening, but I asked her to come over and hinted, "Better wear warm clothes. It's chilly out tonight." I knew that if Audrey wore a halter or shorts or any of her transparent blouses, that would be the end of our friendship where Mama was concerned.

Audrey came over in less than half an hour in a long, comparatively quiet skirt and a white blouse which could have been cleaner. She acted well, reserved, polite and agreeable to everything Mama suggested. Yes, she told Mama, her mother indeed had invited me for dinner and the movie we would see afterward would be suitable.

After she left, Mama, not the least bit fooled, said, "This is not the right kind of friend for you. With all the nice girls in this city, why must you choose someone like that, someone who is too old for you and not right?"

Poor Mama! She knew everything. Yet there was little she could do for us. Mirjana wept no matter how Mama comforted her. Marko, more rude than he'd ever been before, skipped out after dinner even when she said he had to stay home; now I was associating with a girl about whom she said, "This is not a good friend, Danica."

"Mamo, I *promised* I'd go," I said, another tiny lie.

"Well," Mama sighed as she gave in, "if you promised, then go this once. But no more. Afterward, find new friends, Danica, good friends. I don't want you to go with this girl, you understand? If you go with the wrong people, you will become just like them, heaven forbid."

"Thank you, Mamo!" I cried. "How good you are!"

I hadn't expected Audrey's apartment to be impressive, and it was no surprise that the small, dingy building in which she lived was sandwiched in between other unsavory apartments on a narrow side street. When there is little money, one cannot pick and choose among the penthouses. But the Lewis apartment had an abandoned air about it, as though nobody intended to stay there and so there was no use in cleaning it, putting it in order or even airing it out. An unloved place, it smelled of stale smoke, cheap magazines and a blaring television.

For the first time, the *very first time in my life,* I appreciated Mama for insisting that we keep our small basement rooms clean, for tending to her beloved herbs and houseplants that grew even in our poorly lighted living room, and for making it home as well as she could. We used to make fun of my mother in a gentle way for "fussing about her nest," but now I was glad for it.

Audrey's mother sat on the sofa and watched the television. She looked like her daughter, only twenty years older, and harder. The same green eyes squinted as she smoked. Suddenly I felt sorry for Audrey and for the first time began to understand her.

"This is my mother, and Mom, this is Donna. C'mon, Donny. Let's get some clothes on you. You look about thirteen years old in that. Let's dress you up and then we'll have dinner."

She pulled me into her room and flung open a closet door. "Take your pick," she said, almost excited about it. "I promised you, see, and I keep my promise. Anything you want."

"That's nice of you Audrey," I said, hesitating. The closet was crammed with clothes, but I didn't want to touch them. Audrey was beginning to look hurt, so I chose a green skirt with white polka dots, perhaps the quietest of all her clothes, and Audrey begged me to wear a "scoopy jersey" with it. I insisted on wearing my own tailored white shirt, which contrasted with Audrey's black transparent blouse and cerise skirt, but she gave up coaxing me.

"Well, if that's how you feel. Let's get on some makeup. Wish we didn't have to eat with Mom, but well, you know. I'd better go help her."

I stood in the bathroom alone before the chipped mirror. A cockroach darted out of a crack in the wall and disappeared in a corner. From the other room came the sounds of a fight as Audrey and her mother yelled at each other over the blare of the television. Disjointed phrases came through.

"You never did tell me. You know I don't want you going there . . ."

"A' right, a'right. I heard it all before, so shove it."

It was terrible to hear a mother and a daughter fighting with each other.

And who are you to disapprove, Danica? Look at you

there. Is that really you, a girl who lies to her mother, who looks the way you do now? I asked the girl in the mirror who looked so strangely grown up. My fingers trembled as I put on my makeup; a smear of blue paint crossed my eyelid, a smudge of black turned my eyebrows into uneven sooty lines, and my lips were unnaturally red. All that was left of the old Danica was the white cotton shirt and the necklace of glass beads that my father once gave me, the blue beads I always wore. The image in the mirror spoke back to me like a friend.

"It's not too late, Danica. Say you've got a headache. Anything at all, but put your own skirt back on and go home."

At the same time Audrey banged on the door. "What're you doin' in there all this time, Donny?"

I could not insult Audrey by leaving before dinner. But right after I would go, I promised myself. Quickly I wiped off most of the makeup and tried to smile at Audrey as we took our places at the table.

Dinner was set on a bare, scratched table. A carton of chicken from the Colonel's Kentucky-fried was placed on the table along with a loaf of sliced bread, three cans of beer and a plate of potato chips. I hated myself for being picky. If their plates were chipped and cracked, wasn't it true that ours were not perfect? Stop being shocked, I chided myself; who do you think you are?

"We're informal here, no tablecloths, no crystal glassware. I believe in taking it easy, saving work wherever I can," Audrey's mother said.

I smiled politely as if to agree.

"I'll bet Donny here has lots of fancy tablecloths. You should see 'em, Mom," Audrey said, waving a chicken leg around as she talked.

Mrs. Lewis took this as a criticism. "This here isn't

good enough for you, Audrey? You wanna go somewhere else?"

Audrey shrugged her shoulders. "Don't be so touchy," she said, yet she winked at me as if she had scored in upsetting her mother.

"Have more chicken. C'mon. There's a nice piece there, Donny, so help yourself," Mrs. Lewis said, shoving the bucket toward me. I thanked her and accepted it. Her eyes narrowed.

"How long've you been over? You don't say much, do you?" she asked.

"Three months," I said.

"Yeah?" she said. "Listen, that's finger food. It means you can eat it in your hands if you want. Here's paper napkins. You don't have to bother with silverware. See?"

"This is rotten stuff. You know how they raise those chickens? Yech," Audrey said. I could not finish.

At last Mrs. Lewis cleared the table and said, "Guess what I got for you girls, a real treat. In honor of Don . . . what's your name?"

She brought out mugs of coffee and a cherry pie that indeed looked beautiful with a two-inch layer of what seemed to be whipped cream on top. At last I could compliment them honestly. "It looks great. We never have pie like that at home, so it's a treat."

Mrs. Lewis looked pleased at that and cut me a large piece. But it tasted strange; certainly it wasn't whipped cream. Then I remembered Mama telling about how certain commercial pastries were made, and I pecked at it.

"Hey, you don't eat much, do you? What's the matter, you don't like it?" Mrs. Lewis was not at all pleased.

"It's delicious," I lied. "It's just that I had too much chicken."

"H'm," she said, fixing me with her green eyes. "You and Audrey. Two birds, pecking, pecking, pecking!"

"Lay off, Mom," Audrey said. "We have to go now."

"Where you goin'?"

"Around," Audrey said. "To The Cellar maybe, or The Gay Paree."

"What d'you mean, you're goin' there? You're taking this young girl to those places."

"She's not that much younger'n me," Audrey said, getting up.

"Hold on, who's doing the dishes tonight?"

"I'll do them, Mrs. Lewis," I said, although I didn't look forward to it.

"You're the guest. It's up to Audrey, Miss Nose-in-the-Air to do somethin' around here. It's always Mom can do the dishes, Mom get the dinner. Well, you girls go on. Don't get in no trouble. If I were you, I wouldn't go to those places. Y'hear me?"

Poor Audrey! Poor Mrs. Lewis! Poor me, especially poor me. I was suffocating. Pretending I had to go to the bathroom, I pulled off Audrey's skirt, put back on my own short, navy-blue jumper and with a piece of tissue wiped off the rest of the makeup.

"Hey, what's the matter? They aren't gonna let you in with an outfit like that."

"Let's go," I said. I thanked Mrs. Lewis for the dinner and walked out to the street with Audrey. The air was fresh and I breathed deeply and gratefully. But Audrey was furious. Her eyes blazed as she grabbed my coat.

"You can't let me down. You promised you'd go with me. I just want to show you, it's ALL RIGHT. We won't stay long, only a few minutes. And you'll see, the both of us can sing better than most of the people performing now."

"I can't go. I'm sorry, Audrey."

Furious tears filled the green eyes. "I've been waitin' all this time for someone to help me get out of that hole, away from *her,* and you're the one person who can help me and you're backing out."

"I want to help you, Audrey. Honest I do. But not that way. It's not right for me. I don't think it's right for you either. Do something else."

"What?"

"There's a million things you can do. All you have to do is look around."

"I know what I want. Listen, Donny, if you can't come with me, then, please, will you introduce me to Vivienne Marsh?"

She was grasping my arms and I saw in her eyes what I sometimes saw in hurt, wounded animals, an agonized plea. If only her trouble was something simple like a broken leg that could be mended or a sore throat that could be healed, how readily I would have helped her. But her suffering was too deep-seated and too complex for me to handle. I had to help her but didn't know what to do.

"Will you, for heaven's sake, that's all I'm asking, *just introduce me?*"

"I can't, Audrey," I said as gently as I could, "but I'll think of something else. Something better. I want to help you. I swear it, I do."

Her hands fell down to her sides and she walked away. I walked home slowly, aware that somehow I had failed her.

Mama said little but was pleased I had changed my mind and not gone to the movies. There was no need to explain. I played cards with Marko for a while and then helped a pale, tense Mirjana twist paper around wires for an order of flowers she had to finish before the next day.

CHAPTER 25

Audrey never lost hope. I wondered if I should praise her for her persistence or urge her to turn to something else. It surprised me that she still met me in the park and when she felt like singing urged me with a certain sweetness to sing along with her, "just for the fun of it."

At home something else had happened. One day a letter came for Mirjana.

"Be nice to her now," Mama warned Marko and me. "This news from Kalovar may not be the news she wants to hear. Don't say anything."

Mirjana, who now had a job in a factory where she worked long, tiring hours, came in that evening, tired and hot. Mama handed her a cup of hot tea with a spoonful of honey in it. "Take it easy. Rest a while," she said.

"What's all the sympathy about?" Mirjana asked. "I could really use it. I'm done in." She sprawled out on the one upholstered chair. How small she was and how plain she looked with her long brown hair drawn to the back of her head in an old-fashioned bun and the same dull clothes she used to wear in Kalovar. She had been so much prettier there. Poor Mirjana! She still had all the faith in the world that she would soon be going back.

When she finished her tea, she told Mama she would get up and make dinner in a little while. "Just a little rest! That foreman runs us ragged."

None of us could think of anything to say, which puzzled Mirjana, and then she caught sight of the letter on the table where Mama had left it. She picked it up, then noticing we were all watching, said, "Pardon me," and took it into the bedroom.

We waited for the sound of weeping or hysterics, or even a joyful cry in case Mirko had written to say he was waiting for her after all, but there was nothing, not a sound, not a sign.

When Mirjana came out of the room to help make dinner, she neither smiled nor wept. At last my mother dared to ask, "What was in the letter?"

"Mirko and Ana were married last Sunday," she said without expression.

What could we possibly say, that we were sorry, that it was just as well? Mirjana ate calmly and did not say a word all through dinner. Afterward she said she was going for a short walk and when she came home, she went to bed saying nothing more than good night to each of us.

"I'd feel easier if she would only cry a little," Mama confided in me, and I knew what she meant.

The next afternoon Mirjana did not appear at her usual time and Mama worried as she made dinner. Then it was time to eat, but still Mirjana did not come.

"Who can tell what a woman will do when her fiancé marries her best friend? It's a terrible thing," Mama said.

"But Mirjana has so much good sense, you don't have to worry," I said, although I too was worried, for Mirjana always came home on time or called. "Maybe she's at a friend's house."

"Anyhow, let's eat," Marko said.

"We might as well," Mama said absently.

No sooner did we begin our soup, when the door opened and in came a strange young woman, smiling, glowing.

"Well, aren't you going to say anything, or would you rather just eat your soup?" Mirjana said, for of course it was she, but I would never have recognized my dumpy sister! Her hair had been cut—later she corrected me, it had been "styled"—so that it made her look taller and somehow very chic. Someone must have taught her how to apply makeup for she had colors on her face I had never seen before. A manicure. New shoes with heels, exactly the kind I had wanted for such a long time, an attractive new dress that was the color of ivory and looked like silk, and a leather handbag with a jeweled clasp.

This couldn't be Mirjana! It was a beautiful Canadian girl!

Mama clapped her hands. "Let me look at you! Beautiful girl, so pretty, so fine! Mirjana, I never would have dreamed . . ."

"Well, if I'm not going back to Kalovar, I may as well spend some money on myself to begin with. If it's all right with you, I'm going to stay here."

I hugged her. "I'm proud to be your sister!"

"Thank you. You're not so bad either. Something more. I'm going to become a Canadian citizen. And tomorrow I might have even more news, but I can't talk about that yet."

It was still Mirjana, and yet it was a strange new person too. "I feel as though I have just walked out of a prison," she said.

Would I ever get used to this elegant stranger? "I liked you the way you were before all this," I said, suddenly missing the tender, pheasant-hen Mirjana with her brown topknot. Understanding what I meant, she took my hand.

"I know what you mean. It wasn't easy to get my hair cut. But I'm still the same Mirjana. The top dressing has changed, that's all. Anyway, I'm through with weeping and wanting to go back. Now I am *here*."

"Will you go to sing with your friends still, the Pjevaj?" I asked.

"Sure, I wouldn't miss it. Danica, won't you come too and join us?"

I almost said yes but something stopped me. "Maybe sometime. Not now."

The next night when Mirjana came home, she told us she had quit her hated job in the factory and would now be working during the noontime rush and on Saturdays as cashier in a very splendid restaurant.

"See, Mamo. I'm really in training. I'll learn all the secrets of the best restaurants so that when we're ready to begin The New Zagreb, we'll know exactly what to do."

And in the hours when she wasn't working, she told us, she would still be going to college to continue her English courses and concentrate on accounting and business practice.

"When I hear you talk like this," Mama said, "my feet stop hurting and my head stops aching because I know our day will come. We must never stop praying. After all, God may be listening."

CHAPTER 26

Everyone complained that it was a hot summer that year, but Mama, Mirjana and I laughed at the thought of it even as we wiped the perspiration from our brow. We remembered summer in Kalovar when the heat was so thick that the air shimmered above the wheat fields and we could hardly sleep at night. The Canadians did not appreciate how comfortable it was in this place where I was already learning to take along a sweater, "just in case."

More and more people flocked to the beaches and parks in such numbers that they seemed to come from everywhere. Walking along the "Northern Riviera" I picked out those I would have liked to have as friends, this girl here who laughed so easily or that boy lying on the grass reading, because he looked so intelligent, and what fun it would be to know that group of young people who were flying all kinds of kites at the splendid First Beach of English Bay.

But except for the Croatian friends Mama made in another part of the city, we knew few people. Even those who lived in the other apartments of the Villa Rosanna were strangers to us. We nodded and said good morning when we met in the hall, and I sometimes had very short conversations with the very thin English lady who lived in the suite opposite ours or the stout widow who lived on the first floor and kept three Angora cats. In Kalovar we knew everyone.

"Well, no place is as lonely as a city," Dr. Weiss explained one hot afternoon. "You may think of it as loneliness, which is terrible, or you may regard it as privacy, which isn't such a bad idea. Ah, my dear, just the thing!"

Mrs. Weiss was carrying in a tray for us on which were three glasses of cold water made pink and refreshing by the addition of a tablespoon of red wine in each. "If it were all red wine, it would be too strong. A touch is exactly right for a day like this!" Mrs. Weiss explained.

They were hardly my companions, but they were my friends, real friends. My mother baked a large round loaf of holiday bread, fragrant with honey and raisins, especially for them.

"Only a remarkable woman could bake a bread like this," Mrs. Weiss said.

"Only a remarkable woman could have such a daughter as Danica," Dr. Weiss added. "And someday we must all get together and have a little celebration."

"What for?" Mrs. Weiss asked.

"We'll see when the time comes," Dr. Weiss said.

I rose because it was time for me to go.

"You must thank your mother for both of us," Mrs. Weiss said, "for we appreciate her kind gift. I shall write to tell her."

"Yes," said Dr. Weiss, "she is a very gracious lady."

It was good to hear Mama praised, and how pleased she would be when I told her that night.

"Thank you," Mama said. "That is nice to hear. They are kind, your friends."

But it was not what I expected. After dinner Mama sat

at the kitchen table and frowned as she pretended to be doing her English assignments.

"Mamo, if it's English, what are you doing with all those figures on the page."

"It's that kind of an English lesson," Mama lied unconvincingly.

But Mirjana was not satisfied. Sitting beside Mama, she put her hand under her chin and looked into her eyes directly.

"Mamo, you're not telling the truth. Something is bothering you. You can't keep it from us any longer, so tell us. What are those numbers all about, eh?"

"You're sure getting Canadian with an 'eh' after every sentence," I remarked. Mama rubbed her forehead and pretended she didn't understand Mirjana, who spoke English much of the time now and kept encouraging the rest of us to do so too.

"It's only numbers. A little arithmetic. What are you, the district attorney?" Mama asked.

Mirjana was too busy studying the figures to answer. "Mamo, this is the budget, isn't it? Here's our rent, our food. What's wrong?"

At last Mama confessed. The hours that she worked and the pay that she received did not quite work out. "I don't understand. Those weeks when I work overtime, I don't get any more than ordinary weeks. The way it's going, Mirjana, I can't save anything. How can I ever think of opening a restaurant?"

"Let me take a look," Mirjana said. She examined Mama's figures, asked many questions, wrote everything down, nodded and finally came to a conclusion.

"Mamo, darling, you are being had. You know what that means? They are CHEATING you. And that's against the law. So we'll do something about it."

"No, Mirjana, no. If you make a fuss and they find out, they'll fire me and then what will we do? Better make the best of a bad deal and hope for something better another time."

"Mamo, NO. We aren't going to wait for some magic day. Tomorrow we'll go to the Immigration Office and they'll tell us what to do. They won't allow you to be cheated. It would be wrong for us not to do this."

Mama agreed nervously. She took time off from work the next day. "It takes time," she said, worried, but not very much time, for the very next morning she and Mirjana came home grinning in triumph, their arms laden down with big brown bags filled with delicacies.

"Mirjana is right! She should be a lawyer. We won, Danica, we won! The restaurant has to pay me more wages and make up for what they didn't give me before. Have you ever heard of such a thing?"

Mirjana's eyes danced with victory. "It would never have happened like this at home."

We celebrated at dinner with red salmon, new potatoes, fresh blueberries and cream and a splendid yellow cake from the bakery.

"Look out, Canada! The Pavelics are coming!" Marko cried in his high, boyish voice.

They all have had their victories, they are all on their way, I was thinking. Mirjana was becoming a new Mirjana, though in a way she was still the same. Mama was beginning to see her way clear toward getting her restaurant and now that she could speak and understand the new, difficult language better than before, she did not take insults from the men at the restaurant. As for Marko, he had stopped fighting and was earning some money as a paper boy.

Only I foundered about like a fish at the end of a line. "You're lost," Audrey had said. "You're no Canadian, not yet. Trust me. We could be a good team, sing in a good place, make lots of money. Especially if Vivienne Marsh is willing to help. C'mon," she pleaded. "C'mon, Danica. Wake up!"

"Maybe she's right," I thought. "Maybe."

CHAPTER 27

My father once told me it was a sin to be confused. I'm not sure if it's a sin, but I know it's uncomfortable to be caught between decisions.

Mirjana sensed this. I know it now although I couldn't see it then. She urged me to sing with her group and when I said no, more reluctantly this time than before, she told me I could join a Croatian dance group and take part in a big folk festival. "You don't know what fun it is! Too bad you never got to dance in Zagreb, but you can make up for it here."

I wanted to go, yet I wanted more to be thought truly Canadian.

"Don't look so unhappy then," she said when I shook my head no.

If I had some decent clothes, a little money, some friends and, more importantly, a feeling that I was somebody, then I might think of taking part in a festival. The more I thought of Audrey's idea, the more sense it made. I talked with her, insisting on certain points. We would go to a restaurant at first where there was some entertainment, but not a nightclub, certainly not a place where I'd be ashamed to take Mama. We would not ask Miss

Marsh to help us. And we would not wear odd raggedy clothes but would give the impression of being refined yet interesting persons. Audrey objected to this last.

"You can't be refined and 'interesting' at the same time. Being really different, wearing things nobody else would think of, is half the fun," she said, clearly disappointed.

"Then do your own act by yourself. You could, you know."

She must have been very shy or full of fear, because she agreed with everything I said. I reasoned that it would probably work out well; once Audrey began, she would be able to get along without me. Or perhaps we would even be successful and make some money. Of course there might be some trouble when they discovered my true age, but I'd worry about that later.

My head said one thing, my heart another. I practiced songs with Audrey and often wondered if we were any good at all, not quite believing that we were; yet I made no move to find a place where we could audition. Actually, I was hoping she would get discouraged with me and find someone else. But it didn't happen like that at all.

I began to dream, the same dream over and over. Vesna used to tell me that dreams were important because they told us about truths we were afraid to face. Sometimes I understood that and other times my dreams made no sense. This one was all too clear.

I was walking through the woods in Stanley Park, but getting more and more lost. Then Tanja came along and took my hand. "I'll help you, Danica. Come with me." She led me deeper into the woods, away from the path and through the brush which grew so dense and dark I feared I'd never find my way out. Then the girl laughed and laughed until she had to hold her sides, and I could see it wasn't Tanja at all but an evil siprit.

Every time this dream occurred, I awoke trembling. Then foolishly I put it aside, forgetting Vesna's teachings. "It's only a dream," I said, as if it didn't mean anything.

How often I wished that Audrey would forget this compulsion of hers, but no, she met me almost every afternoon. Then she did something which made me so furious, even she would have understood had I told her everything was over between us.

I had never permitted her to go with me to any of my employers' houses, nor did I tell her where they lived, particularly Miss Marsh. Somehow she found out. On that very afternoon when I went to call for Skira, Miss Marsh, lovely in an apricot-colored chiffon dress, said she'd go down on the lift with me as she had to leave early. She chatted easily, telling me about a new trick she was teaching Skira as we walked outside into the late afternoon sun. The smile froze on my face as I looked across the street and saw Audrey waving enthusiastically.

"Yoo-hoo, Donny, yoo-hoo!"

Today she was dressed in black velvet shorts, boots, a tight T-shirt and green felt hat. A wide smear of lipstick stained her mouth. I turned my head, pretending I didn't see her. The tiniest frown appeared on Miss Marsh's forehead as she noticed Audrey, but she said nothing and finished her anecdote. Still, that quick frown of disapproval gave her away and I knew she thought as little of Audrey as had my mother.

"Well, I must go now, dear Danica," she said. How easily she smiled! "Good-bye, Skira! Have a good walk and, Danica, thanks very much for taking such good care of my love."

She walked away toward the garage where she kept her car and I strode resolutely toward the park with Skira, deliberately ignoring Audrey.

"Hey, Donny! Wait up, wait for me. Don't go so fast."

I would gladly have broken into a run even on that hot afternoon, but I had to stop at a red light and she caught up with me.

"I told you never to interfere," I said crossly, "especially with those vile pants. Do you think Miss Marsh would ever look at you now?"

"I thought this outfit would attract her attention, y'know. It's different."

"She saw you all right, too bad for you."

"Come on, Danica, don't be like that. Anyway, the sidewalk's public and if I want to stand there, it's my right," she said, trying to keep up with my pace as I hurried on. It was a new experience having her follow me like this.

"Please, Danica. I'm sorry. I won't do it again."

Skira and I walked straight ahead.

"It's not as if you owned Miss Marsh. I can like her too. She's beautiful, she's . . . you know what I mean?"

I knew. Maybe Audrey was right. Miss Marsh was for me a magnificent secret and what I dreamed of her was so personal I could not tell Audrey or anyone.

"Please, Danica, don't be mad."

I stopped and faced her. She was older than I and had ever so much more experience, yet at that moment she seemed very young and somehow lost, a child who needed someone to like her. I understood it all too well, so I couldn't leave her then; I simply couldn't walk away.

"All right," I said, and we walked into the park together, not talking, not singing.

CHAPTER

28

"If we're going to do this thing, then let's do it,"
I said, "and get it over with." It was another day when
the heat pressed down, making the streets and buildings
shimmer palely.

"You sound as if you were talking about a funeral,"
she said. "You have to be, you know, enthusiastic."

"I'll try to smile."

We knew at least six songs very well and several others
only fairly well, but it was enough for a beginning. We
had agreed to ask the manager of a small restaurant on
Granville Street for an audition; it was not the most elegant place in town, but at least I wouldn't be ashamed to
have Mama see me there.

"You still haven't done anything about something to
wear," Audrey said. "You can't wear that old thing. Jeans
won't be any good for this."

She was right. Even the good "silk" dress that Mama
had made over was more fitting for a ten-year-old than for
me.

We drifted through the park on those hot, hazy days
dreaming of what we should wear. Slinky low-cut dresses?
No, no, not for us. A sweet, long, lacy skirt, Audrey asked.
It could be too much, too sweet, I said and she agreed.

We finally agreed more or less on an image. We would be young, refreshing and interesting, not freakish or wild. Audrey was not entirely pleased, nor was I, but she agreed to scour the city for exactly the right things for us to wear. She knew hundreds of dress shops, she said, little cubbyholes where she could find anything. She was a master at getting bargains.

I wanted nothing more than a new dress, something long, soft and cool. Was Audrey capable of finding it? It hardly seemed possible, but as long as it kept her busy, so much the better.

The unexpected heat wave was wearing me down. Budi and Lancelot dragged along through the park, tongues hanging out, and more often than not they preferred to lie under a cool, leafy bush and pant in lieu of the nice brisk walk they were supposed to take. But the heat charged Skira with even more energy than usual and it was all I could do to hold her leash and keep her from racing free.

Audrey disappeared for a few days and I thought how splendid it would be if she had decided to abandon this silly scheme of hers, but on a stifling Thursday afternoon as I walked along the seawall with Skira toward the entrance to the park, Audrey came running toward me, a scarf floating behind her and her eyes wide and bright. But first she had to talk with Skira.

"Hey, you gonna say hello to me today?" she asked, and as usual Skira turned her head away. "Stinker, she just won't say hello, darn her."

She turned to me more happily. "Guess what, Donny, I've found dresses for us. Perfect dresses. Don't worry, it's a legit store, not far from here. And the owner said if we bought two, she'd give us a real good price."

"I'll see them as soon as I take Skira back."

"Won't do, Donny. The store will be closed by then. Look, she's holding them for us. It's just off Denman Street and I can take Skira's leash while you go in and look."

"I can't do that, Audrey. I'm supposed to be exercising Skira." Yet I was weakening, particularly as Audrey described the dress of salmon pink and white she had chosen for us; I longed to see it. At last I agreed, but insisted it must not take more than a minute of my time away from Skira.

The shop was small but proper, and not far from the park. "Skira, be good now," I said as I reluctantly gave Audrey the leash. Inside a pleasant, motherly saleslady went to get the dress when I explained that Audrey had been in before. I glanced outside where Audrey talked with Skira, but Skira was pawing the ground, not a good sign.

"Here you are, dear!" the woman said, showing me a long cotton dress, so feminine with tiny sprigs of flowers, so delicate with soft ruchings and so exactly perfect that I couldn't imagine Audrey had chosen it. Nor was the price bad at all; why, I could actually afford it.

"Better try it on. It will only take a minute," the saleslady said, and I thought, of course, I can be very quick about such things. I glanced out of the window to let Audrey know that I loved it, but she was bent over, concentrating on Skira, apparently trying to get her attention. As usual, Audrey was smoking and as Skira turned her head, Audrey blew smoke in her face. Immediately Skira jerked away and began to run off in long racing strides.

I shoved the dress back in the saleslady's hand and ran out to chase Skira, fearing it was hopeless to keep up with her. She bounded across busy Denman Street, causing an angry screech of brakes and I followed while two motorists yelled at me.

"Skira, wait up, Skira, Skira!" I called.

Surprisingly enough she stopped at the sound of my voice as if to wait for me. Apparently she thought I was playing, for she wagged her tail and let me approach her, but just as I reached for the leash, she began to run once more in long, graceful strides. She nearly caused another minor traffic jam as she crossed a street and bounded into the park.

"Skira, stop! Please, Skira! Wait for me!"

My English abandoned me and I called her in Croatian, but she understood and waited, silhouetted at the crest of a grassy meadow. About a dozen people who were dozing or sunbathing stared at me, then lay their heads down again as I raced after Skira. Again I almost reached her. She watched me with bright golden eyes and it seemed as if she were laughing at this game we were playing. Breathless and dizzy with heat, I wanted to throw myself down on the grass; never had my heart pounded harder; but Skira was bounding away in a new direction and I had no choice but to get her.

She was heading for the street once more and now I was fearful that the good luck she had had in evading cars so far might not last. I could not bear to think of what would happen if I were to lose Skira! I would never forgive myself. Obviously she was enjoying herself, racing skillfully and swiftly between women with shopping bags, around an astounded party of tourists and through four Pakistani gentlemen who were holding a conference on the sidewalk. Some students yelled at me as I followed Skira.

"Get 'er, girl!"

"Look at 'er run!"

But Skira was not to be captured. She headed toward Georgia Street, a large avenue that feeds into the road that goes to the Lion's Gate Bridge, where there was always a frantic knot of cars, trucks and buses. Skira plunged right through the middle of the intersection, a suicidal thing to do, yet she would have made it to the other side had not a large truck made a sudden terrifying blast with its compressed air horn. This stopped Skira cold so that she froze into position in fear, head lifted, too paralyzed to move. The truck was beginning to move, perhaps in an effort to shock Skira into running again, but she stood motionless. Traffic or not, I ran between the cars, shouted to Skira, and if I'm not mistaken, the sound of my voice brought her to her senses again and she ran to the safety of the sidewalk.

But I was less lucky. My sides were bursting with pain, the air was vibrating with black dots, and I could not move fast enough to get out of the way of a car in the lane beyond the truck. I recall a screeching sound, the harsh gleam of sunlight on metal and an enormous force hurling me to the ground as though in slow motion, taking me hours to fall. Then the brilliant, late afternoon sun was blotted out by a curtain of black velvet that covered me completely.

CHAPTER 29

An image like a bad dream, a row of blank, curious faces looking down on me from above, then Skira breaking through the circle and staring at me, her brow furrowed, incomprehension in the sad, golden eyes. I couldn't understand it and dropped back into blackness.

"Take it easy!" someone cried. I was lifted and carried through burning sunlight to the cool, shaded safety of a long, white car. Ambulance? Hearse?

Everywhere it ached and hurt. I groped for a sign, a word to tell me where I was and what had happened. The answers sank into blackness.

In a cool room now, lying on a table, I was aware of a policeman standing nearby. A woman I did not know bent over me, her face looming large.

"Your name? What is your name? Come now, tell us your name."

They kept asking me and I knew my name must be somewhere. I had to find it, couldn't afford to lose it. "If you lose your name, Danica. . . ." That was my father's voice. Like a white bird my name swooped up out of the darkness and I shouted it triumphantly.

"Danica! Danica Pavelic!"

"Good! Where do you live? Do you have a telephone?"

Too many questions. A voice spilled out the address, and the telephone number rolled slowly off my tongue, each number heavy as a stone.

That was all I could give. Gratefully I drifted into a pain-filled sleep.

"Danica, Danica. Thank God, you are alive."

My mother was there, but where "there" was, I could not tell, only that she sat beside me. I traveled from a planet ten light years away to this place where Mama sat near me and wept.

"I can't see you, Mamo."

Nor could I lift my left hand. But with my right, I felt something dark over my eyes. A bandage? My head was in a strange cap, no, a bandage that was like a cap or a turban. Everything seemed to have a gray fuzz about it, but if I tried perhaps I could step through this gauzy layer. I heard my mother praying to the Virgin to help me.

"Where am I, Mamo? What happened?"

She did not have to tell me. I knew. A sudden fear jerked me upright.

"Mamo, what happened to Skira?"

"Lie down, Danica. She's all right. That Miss Marsh said she trotted home all by herself, but, oh my, she was so worried about you. They promised me, you would be better."

"Mamo!"

Her hand covered mine, not a large hand but strong, very strong.

"Mamo, let me go home with you."

"Later, Danica." That was not my mother's voice but that of a nurse. "We have to keep you here for a short while to make sure everything is all right, and then you can go home."

One minute my head was light as a balloon and the

next it was heavy as a stone. All I knew was that Mama was there and I was weak and sick, helpless as a child. A big child, but still, a child.

"And now," the crisp voice of the nurse continued. "It's time for sleep. Make a fist with your right hand. There, that's a good girl."

"I'm still here, Danica. Go to sleep. Don't be afraid . . ."

While she was still talking, I fell into the blackness, but it was not so deep or so far away as before. This time I slept, knowing I would waken again.

First one doctor came, then another, and still another. One said, "How are you?" and didn't wait for an answer, another said "H'm," and the third, a woman, spoke in a gentle voice, "Danica? You're going to be all right. Don't worry."

They left. And then I heard a familiar voice.

"Well, well, Danica, and what are you doing here?"

"Dr. Weiss!"

"What a scare you gave us, racing across Georgia Street, tying up traffic for miles!" Under the joking tone, I could sense his genuine concern.

"Dr. Weiss, am I going to be blind? Please tell me the truth."

"I don't think so, Danica, but we'll see right now. You're under observation, which means we have to treat you carefully for a while to make sure everything is all right. We were afraid you had a skull fracture but the X-rays look fine. You have a broken arm, but it was a clean break and will mend well. It's amazing that you are alive at all."

As he spoke, clever fingers were untying knots and cutting through the bandages. I opened my eyes and the light blazed in, so I had to shut them fast.

"Very good. Reaction normal," the doctor said. "Let me pull the curtain and shade the room. It may take a while for you to get used to the light."

Now I could make out forms, large white shapes, a few dark areas, and then everything resolved into reality and I could see as clearly as before. The first person my new eyes rested on was Dr. Weiss himself, no longer the short, roundish man with the contemplative eyes I knew before, but someone taller, and more dignified.

"It's all right. I can see!" I said, wanting to laugh and cry at once. It was almost like being born again.

"Good, Danica, good! You are one person too valuable to lose." He sat on a chair by the bed and his eyes never left mine. "Do you want to tell me what happened? Something was not quite right with your life, was it? I was aware of it, and yet, I could not tell."

Somewhere in the blackness certain questions had found their answers.

"I almost made a bad mistake. I wanted to help someone. Now it's clear that I was wrong. Someday . . ."

I could not tell him yet about Audrey. Anyway, the matter was solved, that foolishness was over. He waited, then patted my hand.

"If you ever want to tell me, I will listen. Don't worry about it now. Rest. Get well. Budi misses you, do you know that?"

"Sweet Budi."

"Guess who exercises him every day faithfully? Your brother, Marko. Budi likes him, but when you come back, if you still want your job, it's yours."

"Thank you. You are very good to me."

"You are a person who should be looked after, because, Danica, you are very special. We'll talk of this later, all right? I must go now—other patients. Rest well."

The nurse arranged my pillows after he left and I lay

back watching the beams of sunlight that floated through the air. I sipped a glass of orange juice. A bird settled on a branch of a tree, his shadow outlined on the drawn curtains; then he flew away.

How good it was to be alive again!

When I awoke that afternoon, Mama was sitting by my bed.

"How are you, Danica?" She looked more tired and worried than ever.

"I'm getting well, Mamo. Dr. Weiss is looking after me. But Mamo, you're exhausted. I didn't mean to make all this trouble. Mamo, I've been very selfish. I'm sorry. Forgive me."

"God forgives, Danica. So I must too."

It could have been the first time I really saw my mother and understood what courage she had to give up the home she had always known to come to this strange country, to wrestle with a difficult language, and care for all of us by herself. As if that were not enough, now I caused her this new anxiety. She was bending over, rubbing her ankle.

"Mamo, are you tired? Your feet hurt?"

"My heart hurts more to see you lie there in that bed in a hospital. Dr. Weiss tells me they treat you nice, the very best. But when you come home, everything will be all right, eh?"

"Everything will be wonderful. Mamo, someday you'll be proud of me. Wait and see . . ."

Another promise, Danica? But this time I would not fail.

Mirjana brought me flowers, real flowers this time, fragrant red roses. Marko, cleaned and polished for the visit, stood beside her, restrained and tense in these unfamiliar surroundings.

"Danica, is that you under those bandages?"

"Sure, who else would it be?"

"Hey, I'm sorry about you getting run over and all that," Marko whispered, his eyes bugging out as though I were already a corpse laid out in a coffin with the candles burning around me.

"That's okay. How's the baseball coming?"

"Fine. Danica, I'm taking care of your dogs, but only until you're better. I'm saving your job, see? That Skira is really some dog."

"I'll bet Miss Marsh thinks you're cute."

Marko actually blushed and turned away. She must have made him feel quite grown up. And now Mirjana chattered. It seemed as though I'd been away from home . . . yes, Vancouver was now "home" . . . for months.

"I've joined the Croatian group and I'll be dancing in the Festival this year. It's a marvelous group, as good as the one in Zagreb."

Zagreb seemed far away, yet it was only a year ago that I had almost danced there.

"Maybe next year you'll change your mind and dance with us. What do you think?"

"If they take me, Mirjana. If I still remember the steps."

"You'll remember all right. It's in your blood, Danica. You'll never forget."

She was right. It was part of me and I would never forget it, never again. The nurse, hearing the last of our conversation, said I'd better wait a few days before dancing and it was time for visitors to leave.

My bed was in a small ward, but the curtains were kept drawn to keep me quiet until all the tests and X rays were complete. To my surprise, Audrey came to visit one afternoon. She swished into the room with a long skirt, sleazier than any I'd ever seen on her, a brief, low-cut jersey and the straw hat with even more straws missing from it now. She perched on the end of the chair beside the bed and stared down at me. Once I thought she could have been pretty; now she gave the impression of being off-key, like a song sung out of tune. She became arrogant again, as when I first knew her.

"Well, Donny, I guess it's all over for us, isn't it?"

"Not for you, Audrey. It wasn't really right for me anyway. You'd probably do better by yourself without me, in your own style."

"I don't know."

"You mustn't be discouraged."

"If we'd had the breaks, if you hadn't been so stubborn about Miss Marsh . . ." she broke off, walked to the window and turned around, more humble now, her eyes moisting a little. "I'm sorry about what happened, letting Skira get away. Lord, you could've been killed."

"Well, I wasn't. And anyway, I should have held on to that leash myself, so it's more my fault. Anyway, it's over and no tragedies, so we're lucky. Don't look so sad, Audrey."

"Everything could've worked out," she insisted. "I've got such rotten luck."

Before I could say anything, the nurse scurried in, excited. "Another visitor for you, Danica. Look pretty now. Here, I'll get another chair."

I heard a buzz of excitement in the hall and saw several nurses whispering together. My heart jumped; it was Miss Marsh! She smiled at the nurses and walked over to me, handsome in a creamy silk dress with a patterned scarf tied around her head and a large straw bag. She also carried an intriguing gift package, soft gray paper held down with gold ribbons.

"My dear girl, dear Danica, what a dreadful thing has happened! How are you feeling now?"

"All right."

"I've been so upset about you and was so relieved to hear that you are going to be well again. Skira sends her love; you can be sure of that."

"Miss Marsh, I feel so awful about what happened. I tried to catch Skira but it was almost impossible. I was so worried until I heard that she was all right."

"She's fine. I know what happened. You were very brave to try to save her. Don't think I don't appreciate that. What I don't understand is how she got away. But I guess it was just an accident."

Audrey had sunk into the corner. Her face turned ashen white, but she had no need to worry. I wasn't going to give her away.

"It just happened. I'm sorry, Miss Marsh."

"Well, the important thing is that you're all right," she said, and Audrey sighed in relief.

"Miss Marsh, I want you to meet my friend, who wants to be a singer. This is Audrey Lewis, Miss Marsh."

"How do you do, Audrey?" Miss Marsh held out her hand to Audrey, who gulped, shook hands awkwardly and mumbled a few polite words.

"Here's your chance, Audrey," I said, never dreaming she could be so shy and so utterly miserable that it was clear she couldn't say a word. Miss Marsh put her at ease by turning to me.

"I must dash off, but I simply had to see you. This is for you," she said, giving me the package. "Perhaps Audrey can help you open it, unless you can manage with one hand. I'll see you again. Get well now, Danica."

"Thank you, thank you for coming."

After she left, Audrey came over to the bed. "I never

saw anyone so beautiful. Thank you for introducing me. But I just couldn't say a word."

I had introduced her at last, given her what she had always wanted, and nothing came of it. She stood hesitantly by my bed.

"Audrey, what's going to happen to you?"

"I don't know. Maybe I'll move on, to Toronto, or Montreal."

"Maybe you could go back to school, train for a good job, get some money and even have your own place, a shop or something. Don't you ever think of it?"

"Who, me? Don't be silly. Work is a bore. Why don't you open your present? I guess I should've brought you something."

"I'm glad you came. That's enough."

Miss Marsh's gift was a bottle of French perfume and a card in her own generous handwriting. The perfume was heavenly. "Here, try it, please, Audrey."

She let me anoint her ear tips with this precious scent. For a second she looked happier, then stood up.

"Good-bye, Donny. Danica. That's what you wanted me to call you, isn't it? For a while it was great being with you and dreaming. Hopeful, y'know?"

"Audrey, things could work out for you if you let them."

She shook her head, pulled down her hat and said, "So long," in a hopeless kind of voice. Then she left.

I had visions of her drifting from one place to another and still another in a slow, downward spiral, and I wondered if I'd ever see her again.

CHAPTER 30

With the long hours stretching out before me, there was time to think, to wonder and to remember. It was almost a year ago that my father had died a needless death and again I felt the anger within me for not having been able to help him. I had made a vow and forgotten it.

A girl who had been wheeled into the ward after a long, complicated operation groaned in pain from time to time. I could not see her because of the curtain that separated her bed from the rest of the ward. But I sensed her pain all through the day and then again all through the night. And I knew that I wanted to help her. The next morning she was moved to a private room, but I could not forget her anguish.

When Dr. Weiss came to examine me and to tell me the good news that in a few days I could go home, he stopped mid-sentence. "I should think you would be delighted, but you look so solemn!"

"Could I talk with you for a minute or two?"

"Surely," he sat down and waited. He looked nothing like my father but at that moment it was almost as if he were my father. I told him briefly about what my father's life had been and how he died and how I had made an oath to become a doctor, and then how I had forgotten it because it seemed so hopeless.

"Hopeless, but why?"

"I was looking for something else, something different. But now I want to know, in this country, is there any chance for me?"

"Do you care enough? That is the whole secret. To care enough to work hard for a long time, even when you're tired, even when it's not easy. That is the most important thing of all. As for talent, now I have a confession to make to you. I've been hearing about how you used to cure animals back in Kalovar, and once you helped Vesna deliver a baby, and you cured a dog that even the vet had given up for lost. So, I would say that is a good recommendation."

"But I don't speak English well and we don't have money for med school."

He gestured with his hand as if that hardly mattered at all. "If you want to do this, if there is a cry within you that never stops, then nothing will keep you from becoming what you think it is your fate to be."

A nurse came in the door with a message for Dr. Weiss. He got up to leave. "In the Bible it says, 'Rejoice in your work, for that is your portion.' I'll see you later, Danica."

After he left I thought of what a strange pattern had been unfolding. If poor Audrey only believed in herself, she might be a singer. She had her wish; she had met Miss Marsh, and yet it came to nothing. I knew without doubt that Mama would get her new restaurant, one way or another, because Mama believed. All one had to do was discover the right path. Now it seemed as though everyone was helping me to do this whether or not they knew it. How fortunate I was!

A pillow sailed past me in the middle of this reverie,

bringing me back to the present, and laughing now, I threw it back as well as I could to Margaret, another patient in the ward who had broken her leg mountain climbing but sang and talked of nothing else but the next mountain she was going to climb. Another girl, Sheila, lay quietly with a fever that wouldn't come down. The fourth bed was empty.

That night a table was wheeled into the room and two orderlies placed a girl on the bed. She lay there still and white, the odor of anesthesia hovering above her. A nurse came in to see that she was all right.

"What happened?" Margaret asked.

"Emergency appendix," the nurse said, "but she's doing fine."

She lay there white and still, seemingly more dead than alive, her face quiet and pure. But soon she would be well, talking and perhaps joking with Margaret, ready to take up her life again.

What a miracle! There was hope in the world after all. I knew it now. I knew it.

Within two days six bouquets of flowers surrounded Patricia of the burst appendix. Margaret bounced around the ward on crutches and held out a box of candy to the rest of us, although she was careful to hide it when the nurse passed by. Even Sheila was coming back to life.

"It's more like a party in here than a hospital ward," Miss Schilling, the dour head nurse commented. "This is not a social occasion."

I received flowers from Uncle Ivo, a flower-sprigged nightgown from Budi and a gift package wrapped in practical brown paper.

"Open it!" the girls cried as I could not imagine who would send me a gift. A note explained it.

Dear Danica:

I hope you will get well soon and come back to us. Marko performs his duties well, but I do believe that Lancelot misses you.

> *Sincerely,*
> *Agatha Hornby*

The gift was a book, *The Young Lady's Guide to Proper Etiquette*. All three girls haw-hawed at this with shrieks of laughter. Patricia said her aunt gave her a book exactly like it. "You'd better study it. Miss Hornby'll test you on it, I'll bet!"

On my last full day in the hospital, Dr. Weiss asked me if I felt well enough to accompany him through one of the wards. "Only if you want to," he added unnecessarily.

I sat up so fast my head hurt. I put on my robe with certain awkwardness because of my broken arm and together we walked to a ward where six little girls were lying down. Correction: Five little girls were lying down and the sixth was bouncing up and down on her bed.

"What are you trying to do, go through the roof?" Dr. Weiss asked of the small, black-haired Chinese girl who froze the second she saw him and then grinned when she realized he wasn't really angry.

"Lie down, Susan, and let's see what we have here."

He pressed her stomach with his fingers. "There, does it hurt here? In this place? How about here?"

"You're tickling me," she squealed.

"Then I guess we haven't any choice but to say good-bye," Dr. Weiss said. "Here's a girl who's ready to go home."

The others were less fortunate. A small girl whose eyes were so swollen she could hardly open them lay moaning, bruises everywhere on the delicate body.

"Mommy," she moaned.

"It's not Mommy. It's the doctor, Francie. Oh my, we're going to have you all fixed up so you'll feel better soon. All better." Dr. Weiss kept talking gently with the child as he examined her.

"I want Mommy."

Later the doctor told me that this was a battered child.

"A 'what'?" I had never heard of such a thing.

Dr. Weiss explained that the mother had nearly killed her child in a brutal beating and now she was in prison.

"What will happen to Francie?"

"Poor darling. Chances are that she will become a ward of the state. She'll go to an institution or be put out for adoption or a foster parent will take over. It's not an easy world, Danica."

We went from one bed to the next, from those who could hardly wait to get home because they were nearly well to one small child who lay silent and still.

"My dolly fell on the floor," she said quietly. I picked it up for her. She lay calm and resigned as Dr. Weiss examined her, chatting easily with her to put her at ease.

"What a sweet child!" I said as we left the ward.

"Sweet as a flower, that lovely little girl," he said, but I knew there was more he could tell me.

"What's wrong with her?" I asked.

He drew in his breath sharply and hesitated. "If I tell you everything now, Danica, there won't be much for you to learn at med school, will there?"

So I understood that that child, "sweet as a flower," would most likely not go home, nor would she be playing with her dolly much longer.

"There now, Dr. Pavelic, that should be enough for one morning," Dr. Weiss said as we returned to my ward. "Remember, tomorrow morning I come to say good-bye!"

"Thanks."

I was so overwhelmed with what I had just seen, that I almost stumbled over Margaret who was doing her yoga and challenged me to join her.

The day was to bear still more revelations. I found a new word to describe what happened that day—epiphany —which means suddenly understanding something which has been in front of you all along.

Mama came to see me every night during the visiting hours, but it was Mirjana who stopped in the doorway that evening, beckoned to someone with her finger, and then walked in with the girls of her singing group, Pjevaj! They all grinned broadly knowing they not only surprised me but the other girls in the ward who were open-mouthed as well.

Great! I was thinking to myself. If they sing as loud here as they did at their rehearsal, they'd wake all the patients out of their anesthesia as they lay on operating tables. But they gathered around my bed and sang softly, just loud enough so that the other girls in the ward could hear them too.

First they sang a song about the morning star rising pure and sweet, a star that would bring blessings. This old song was about my name and I bowed my head to thank them for it.

Their second song was a familiar one, sung on Jurjevo, St. George's Day, which is when we welcome spring in Croatia and promenade, carrying branches of trees in our hands. And now, because I always loved this song, I found myself singing with them. It was part of me, just as I was a part of Croatia and always would be, even though I was Canadian too.

As I sang, the ridiculous problem that had bothered

me for so long simply fell away. I was Croatian, of course, and nothing would ever change that or the love that I had for my native land. At the same time I was Canadian, and there was no question but that I would love my new country too. Whatever conflict existed had only been in my head. Never again would I be confused.

As we sang, Mama, laughing now, walked in with a large cake and Marko trailed behind her.

"It's time for a celebration because everyone has been so nice," Mama said. The girls still sang softly, but some of the nurses looked in, and for everyone there was a piece of what Mama called Celebration Cake.

Finally the head nurse bustled in, prepared to scold Mama. "This is a *hospital*. There are *sick* people here. Visiting hours were over *ten minutes ago!*"

"It's only a little music, a little piece of cake. Here, please, Nurse, here is some for you."

"Well!" The nurse looked around the room. For a little while anyway, everyone was smiling, everyone was happy. "All right this time, but that's all."

She needn't have worried. The next afternoon I went home. Completely cured!

CHAPTER 31

End of October. The leaves were twirling down, the golden leaves of the maples mingling with the red, the sweetheart leaves of the poplar trees and the bronze and purples of the hickories and oaks, all scudding in the wind to cover the sidewalks and lawns in an ever-changing mosaic. I longed to put down my schoolbooks—nothing is heavier than a chemistry text unless it's math —and run through the leaves, stirring them up with a delicious, crunchy sound.

But there was no time for play. I was fourteen now and had other things to think about, so I held on to the books and only scuffled through the leaves on the way home. Two important tests would face me the next day and I had to do well, because Dr. Weiss would be sure to grill me on what I'd been learning and how I was getting along. Nor could I complain if the work was difficult because after all it was my choice. Nobody ever said it would be easy.

In September we had moved from the basement of the Villa Rosanna and we weren't even living in the West End any more, that Riviera of the North, that city of towers, which I left with a certain regret although it is easy enough for me to take a bus and go back there whenever I wish.

Now we live in a house in East Vancouver where the houses are built of wood with slanted roofs, gables and porches, hardly impressive but sweetly human, like the modest leftover houses I liked so much in the West End. There are small lawns in front of each house, and Mama is already planning the garden she will make next spring in back of the house. Living here is not at all like living in Kalovar, but then it's not like the West End either. It is something new for all of us.

Two and a half blocks away on an important street is The New Zagreb. For so long it was only a dream, such a faraway dream, we hardly dared to think of it. Yet it is now one month old, our own restaurant. At least it will be our own once Mama finishes paying Uncle Ivo his share of the investment in it.

It was at the beginning of September that he telephoned Mama. "Nadja, I'm coming right over to see you. I think I've got the place!"

At the moment I was in the park folk-dancing, so I didn't hear Mama's protests, fears, screams of delight and a never-ending string of prayers. Uncle Ivo said the restaurant that had been there did so well that the owner had moved to a downtown location, a sign that this was a good place for us to start. Thanks to Uncle Ivo's "gonnections" and uncanny business sense, he was able to bid on this place. "You'll never do better, Nadja," he promised.

It was a miracle that The New Zagreb was able to open within a month. Mirjana—that sly fox—was acquainted with any number of artists, art students, carpenters and other young men who would do anything for her, so there was an intense sawing of wood and hammering of nails and smell of paint as The New Zagreb was created. All Mirjana's sketches, which had only been regarded by us as silly daydreaming, now made it possible for the work to go quickly. The platform she designed, the thatched roof above, and the small wooden stairway that really lead nowhere but a painted window and real wooden shutters, took on an air of charm. A small balcony with a red, woven cloth hanging over it and five pots of blooming geraniums suggested the Inn we had in Kalovar.

Of course the murals are not yet finished, but the young artist who has sketched murals of people in Croatian costume folk-dancing, promises it will be finished on Monday when we close for a day. How curious it is that he has a long, black mustache and somehow makes me think of my father. He keeps asking Mirjana if she likes this color or that flourish, anything at all to get her attention and sometimes I catch her sitting and watching him paint.

"Is beautiful, these paintings, the weaving, the decorations on the walls, everything," Mama said, "but remember, people come here to eat, to feel at home and to enjoy."

She worked day and night to get the kitchen exactly as she wanted it to be with Marko and me helping. We thought it would never be ready to open, and yet on the chosen day, The New Zagreb opened its newly decorated doors to the public.

We all work. I wait on tables for two or three hours every night, wearing the white country shirt and blue skirt with its striped apron that Mirjana designed. But at eight-thirty on school nights, Mama insists that I change back to my jeans, go home and concentrate on my studies.

On Mondays the restaurant is closed, which is perfect

for me because that is when the folk-dance group meets. I was torn between that and the choral group, so I flipped a coin and it came out dancing. Once the music begins, my feet want to move. "Mamo, I could dance forever!" I tell her, but she answers that she has more sensible ideas for me.

We live in the top story of an ordinary wooden house painted a rich brown. It is not an outstanding piece of architecture in any way, and yet it feels like home in a way that the Villa Rosanna never did. From our windows we can see into the branches of maple trees and, beyond that, the triangles of roofs on other houses that are much like ours, while the high blue mountains of the north are a strong and silent backdrop for all the city.

Mama dreams of her garden. "It won't be like the one we had before because it's too far north for almonds and lemons, but we can have apple trees, a plum tree, some blueberries and tons of vegetables, all we can eat."

Marko, who is studying woodwork in school, wants to build a chicken coop and a rabbit hutch. "And beehives, Mamo. We gotta have bees and honey! Like we did before."

"All in good time," Mama says. "Now that our feet are on the ground at last, we can begin to build toward heaven."

On this October day, just as I have resisted the urge to drop my books and run through the leaves, my friend, Alice, dashes up the street and yells for me to wait. Though the wind is blowing damp and it's getting cold, we stand around and talk for a few precious minutes about the skirt she is going to make, about who is the best-looking boy in the class (her problem not mine), and Please, Danica, won't you join the Glee Club at school.

"I'd love it, Alice. I'm dying to learn all kinds of songs. If you could lend me an extra hour or two each day . . ."

There's no time for singing this year because I must still study English. I am improving, but still I make too many mistakes. And there is not enough time because I must work in the restaurant, and I am happy to do this. If I am to get a scholarship to medical school someday, then now I must study hard. So one night of folk dancing is my delight and indulgence, the only one I can afford.

"Alice, I can't stay any more. Wish I could, but you understand . . ."

Alice is a good friend and she does understand.

As I change into my waitress blouse and skirt, the phone rings. It is Mrs. Weiss inviting me to lunch on Saturday if I can get away. She and the doctor have invited several of their young friends and she would like me to meet them. I promise I will come if I can get Marko to take my place for a few hours.

At the restaurant Mama insists that I have a good dinner before I wait on table. Tonight there is a good crowd, but she calls me into the kitchen at eight-thirty. "Danica, you have exams tomorrow? Then go home and study. That comes first. And thanks for helping. I'll see you later."

It is amazing that Mama never seems tired in the same way she did before, although she works longer hours.

I rush home, holding my coat wrapped tight because the wind is growing cold and bitter. The kitchen, however, is warm, and I sit down at the table to study.

Marko watches television in the living room and I am tempted to sit there with him. Then I remember that Alice invited me to her house; other friends will be there and they will make cookies, gossip about school and get silly. I'm tempted to go, but still I sit at the kitchen table with my books.

There is a vow I made on a hill in Kalovar. I think of the tiny child who will never leave the hospital alive and of Audrey who is ill in another way. Then it is time to shut out the sounds of the television and turn to chemistry. It is not easy, I tell you, and math seems only remotely connected with what I must do, but I accept this without question. It is time to study.

A